The Enlightened Canine

---◦◦◦◦◦---

Jose Perez

The Enlightened Canine

ISBN: 9798880396580

Acknowledgement

I would like to express my gratitude to Robin Ethan for his valuable and helpful assistance for making possible the editing and publishing of this book.

For:

Nickie Perez
Leon Dennis
Robin Ethan
Kacey Natalia
Haley Marcella
Adrian Joseph

The Enlightened Canine

Jose Perez

Table of Contents

LUCKY

When Lucky came into the world, he did it in the lap of luxury. His mother, a single mom, was a provider par excellence. For that reason, there was all sorts of imported clothing in his cradle, not because she disdained the local garments; no, she could allow herself that luxury although she had six little ones.

Lucky had in his cradle an Armani suit, a pair of original Reeboks, Armani underwear, a pair of Ray-Ban sunglasses, and a fistful of dollars.

One could say then that Lucky and his siblings had a small treasure in their possession, yet those were little toys to them. As soon as their bellies were full of maternal milk, they would let go of the teat, signifying the start of the formal events.

The formal events in this family consisted of rear end and mouth licking, and tireless tail wagging. The last formal event was to ceremonially walk their mom to the exit of the small cave that was their home. There she proceeded to lick their adorable little faces and to nibble tenderly and lovingly on their ears, which was her way of saying goodbye. Immediately after that, she descended the steep and dangerous slopes of the ravine that was her territory.

Before disappearing completely, she always turned around to take one last look toward the small cave entrance. Most of the time, Lucky was the only one there to see her disappearing act. Meanwhile, Lucky's siblings had begun the baby doggy Olympic games, Greco-Roman wrestling, running, boxing, a growling competition, high jumping, and finally the competition to see who could strike the litter's weakling to the ground first.

Inadvertently, these games prepared them for the life of feral dogs they would lead as soon as their mother weaned them, and they would have to fend for themselves. But they would worry about that when the time came. For the time being, they had food, toys, a place to sleep, and great playmates. What else could a flea-infested dog want?

As soon as they finished ripping the dollars, and playing tug of war with the credit cards, the shoes, and the underwear, the pups look for their favorite sibling to share some warmth and have a siesta.

Peregrino's favorite sibling was Lucky, the strongest and the chubbiest of them all. Lucky was white and had a black spot on one side of his body in the shape of a horseshoe, a symbol of good fortune—hence his name.

Lucky had a great love for Peregrino. Possibly because he was too small, the weakling of the litter. He was the one that was always sick to his stomach and the one that always got the skinnier teat with almost no milk in it.

Peregrino was the weakling who wailed when his siblings pinned him to the ground. Lucky was always ready to make the bullies run for their lives. That done, he always went to kiss his little brother and lick his face tenderly. Peregrino's little heart could not hold in all the love he had for his big brother. As soon as weariness brought sleep to his eyes, he usually went to Lucky, licked his face, and laid down next to him. Lucky then tenderly placed his head on top of his little brother and surrendered into the arms of Morpheus.

Lucky dreamt that morning for the first time in his life. And something extraordinary happened. He dreamt he was flying. Wings sprouted from his neck rather than his back. Lucky felt an intense pressure there, but it did not bother him; he liked it.

Lucky rose into the air in his dream, but when he was enjoying it the most, he heard screams of panic, shrieks of terror.

When Lucky recognized Peregrino's shrieking, at once he wanted to run and help him, but the charm of his dream and the pleasant sensation of freedom were more substantial than the urge to help his brother. So, he kept flying and dreaming.

As Lucky flew out of the small cave, he caught a glimpse of the deep ravine. *What a wonderful sight,* he thought. The shrieks of uncontrollable terror of his other siblings had joined those of Peregrino. Lucky opened his eyes, startled. He was completely awake and alert; why then was he able to continue flying, he wondered.

As Lucky looked toward the small cave entrance, the last thing he saw was his siblings' faces transfigured by the terror that had taken possession of their little hearts.

Lucky still did not understand what was happening, but his heart stopped. He urinated and soiled himself and was petrified when he looked up. A giant monster had him by the scruff of his neck. Lucky screamed in fear, shaking his body with all his might, trying to release his neck from that hairy claw. As a reward for his great effort, he got smacked hard across his face. The shock and the fear drained all his energy, and he hung lifeless from the claw.

PEPITA

Pepita, the mother of the puppies, was three hundred meters down the ravine negotiating step by step the most dangerous face of the steep slope that her shortcut traversed. She took that dangerous shortcut to get to the bottom of the ravine. It was her daily trek to get to the sacred water her body needed to make the milk to feed her babies.

At the bottom of the semi-vertical wall Pepita was climbing, there were two rows of pointed, sharp, and rain-stained rocks.

Those rocks seemed to be moving away from the wall and from each other, forming an inverted letter V that, seen from Pepita's point of view, appeared to be the lower jaw of a giant fearsome beast.

Pepita could take the safest way to descend to the bottom of the ravine to drink the water she needed, but that took too much time and too much effort, for the simple reason that the safest way traversed the garbage dump.

The garbage dump was a long and wide slope sandwiched between two high and natural walls. One of those walls divided Pepita's steep slope and the garbage dump. The garbage dump was as expected, full of garbage and all types of food leftovers.

There were all sorts of discarded cooking utensils made of plastic or metals, as well as old beds and mattresses. There were many motorcycles and bicycle skeletons, including the rusted body of a 1960s Volkswagen beetle.

Getting through all those obstacles was painfully slow. So, Pepita sooner risked her hide on the dangerous face of the semi-vertical wall than walk through the garbage dump.

The semi-vertical wall measured roughly some twenty meters in height and offered little help to get a paw hold. It was on that wall when Pepita was returning from the small pond after she had assuaged her thirst with the vital liquid, that she heard the shrieks and wails of her babies' terror.

She stopped dead in her tracks, pricked up her ears, and focused them in the direction of the small cave. Yes! She was sure those were the shrieks of her beloved babies.

Pepita forgot about the danger she was in and, as surefooted as a mountain goat, climbed the wall in a few quick leaps and did not stop till she was at the entrance of the cave. There she was arrested for one-thousandth of a second by an unbearable stench. Instantly after that, she stormed furiously into the shelter with her fangs unsheathed.

Pepita returned to the lair to find all but one of her babies. She saw them milling around terror-stricken, and some of them tried hiding behind the others. By the time the babies realized that Pepita had entered the lair, she was gone.

The awful smell she found in the small cave was ingrained in her nose. Pepita climbed like a flash of lightning the twenty meters from her lair to the slope's summit, trying to catch up with whatever took her baby.

Her rabid dog's erratic fast pace brought her face to face with the assassin of street dogs. The insatiable bone crusher. How many dogs had it killed? Nobody knew, nobody kept score, but way too many dogs had fallen under those terrible, fast-moving jaws.

Many friends and some of her siblings, including her mother, had fallen victim to the horrible jaws of death. Pepita herself had many times been dangerously close to being crushed by the six-lane highway called the Periferico.

Street dogs were constantly trying to cross the highway and were always being killed by the speeding vehicles. That road had been swallowed whole by the relentless advance of the concrete jungle and its intertwined streets and avenues.

There she was, facing the Periferico. The unpleasant smell that had taken her baby led her to that dangerous place.

Legs shaking and heart pounding, face to face with the treacherous highway, she waited for any opportunity to run across. The kind of opportunity that a couple of cars keeping their distance could have offered her. Unfortunately for Pepita, most of the vehicles traveling there were going too close to each other as if they were hooked train wagons.

Every time Pepita crossed the highway's six lanes, a black dog materialized out of thin air next to her. That morning was no exception. That extraordinary dog was elegant, beautiful, had a svelte body, and was long-limbed. But it was an insidious and extremely evil being as well, a ghost with the power to appear and disappear at will, known as Guapo and whose good looks were a warning sign.

Pepita cast a sidelong glance at him and turned her face the other way, pretending she had not seen him. But it was a futile effort, because before she turned her face the other way, her heart had fallen prisoner to fear, since she knew perfectly well what that dog represented.

Fear made her lose her sense of survival, and she sprinted across the highway. She didn't look, didn't wait any longer for that slim chance that would allow her to reach the other side without losing her life.

The beautiful black dog was effortlessly crossing the highway next to her. It was moving with the elegant gait of a well-trained Afghan hound in a dog show.

While the black dog was showing off, Pepita was at full speed dodging the speeding fire chariots, as well as the horn blaring and the blaspheming of the drivers. A bus driver cursed when he failed to make a small bloodstain rug with a tail out of her.

When Pepita reached the other side of the highway and remembered to breathe again, her sense of smell immediately picked up the sharp reek that carried Lucky away. She followed that pungent smell, and it took her through the streets and alleyways of an immensely large and impoverished poor neighborhood, known as a barrio.

At the end of the trek, she came to a long, noisy street market.

The pungent smell she was following got mixed up with the fragrance of the flowers and the aroma of the season's fruits and the spiced foods cooked there. Not to mention the sweet and sinful aroma of the nanche, or Byrsonima Crassifolia, that was in its second week of harvest.

When she completely lost the stench she was following, she went around and through the market, over and over, trusting her eyes and her canine ears, but it was to no avail.

The rest of the day, she remained around the market, hoping deep in her heart that somehow her baby would suddenly appear.

When Pepita realized that the sun had long departed from the zenith and was beginning to sink into the horizon, she knew she had lost her baby. Sad and with a profound and overwhelming feeling of helplessness, she returned to her den where five hungry and scared babies waited.

If Pepita had been a human mother of the barrio, she would not have fared better. Because there, human babies are kidnapped as well.

When Pepita finally arrived home, the sun was already behind the mountains. When the babies felt her coming in, their souls returned to their bodies, and immediately all of them ran to hug and kiss her, twisting their bodies and wagging their tails rapidly and tirelessly.

Pepita threw herself to the ground exhausted, and the babies, wasting no time, grabbed a teat each and drained the milk and the little energy she had left. Pepita relaxed her body and instantly, an intense flash of light blinded her.

At the same time, a tremendous pressure took hold of her body, as she was pulled into the realm of dreams in a single and powerful sucking as if she was a strand of hot spaghetti.

The puppies' mother's milk warmed their bodies. The deep sense of security she offered them when she was home, plus the overwhelming feeling that took over their entire beings right after they satisfied heir hunger, hunger that was eating them alive, made the babies succumb to sleep.

Peregrino tried unsuccessfully to find Lucky in the cave's darkness. When he could not find him, making a super canine effort to overcome his fear, he went out of the cave. Once outside, he howled plaintively, calling for Lucky for a long while.

In a pause in his sorrowful howl, he heard a strange noise creeping toward him. Scared, he ran to seek refuge for himself between his mother's front legs. There he fell asleep, and at once he found himself in a dream.

He dreamt he was in an abstract world that got into his eyes incomprehensibly. Suddenly, right in front of his eyes, a good number of parallel and iridescent lines crisscrossed each other, and after that, those lines started performing a beautiful butterfly's dance. When he tried to touch them, the lines vanished. As soon as the lines vanished, he saw an amorphous and iridescent figure that came slowly floating in the air toward him.

"It is me, Lucky," the figure said.

"Lucky! Lucky!"

exclaimed Peregrino as he excitedly ran to hug him, but like the butterflies, the amorphous figure vanished, and Peregrino was left there listening to the echo of an "I love you!" that ricocheted off the walls and ceiling of the small cave.

THE GARBAGE DUMP AND THE JUNGLE

When the babies woke up the following day, they realized that Pepita was gone. Her inseparable friend, hunger, and the urge to drink the vital liquid that her body demanded to produce the milk for her babies had awakened her before dawn.

Before Pepita began the treacherous descent to the bottom of the ravine, she checked the surroundings of her lair to make sure that the awful smell that had taken Lucky was not around and waiting for her to leave. That time Pepita took the long hike that traversed the garbage dump, hoping to find some scraps to eat before her gastric acids consumed her.

Halfway to the bottom, she found a large advertising poster showing Guatemala's city mayor's photograph and his famous slogan: "Put garbage in its place!" On top of the poster, she found the mangled body of Tyson, the pit bull, terror of dogs and children alike, and the most recent victim of the highway.

She sniffed Tyson's body thoroughly, making sure he was dead. Before continuing her long walk, she squatted down and urinated and defecated on the mayor's freckled face. Her masterpiece finished, she continued the descent to the bottom of the ravine.

When she finally reached the ravine's bottom, she began the long trek across all sorts of narrow, dangerous, and bottomless crevices. When at last the ravine's end was in sight, she was very thirsty and dog tired.

The ravine ended at the foot of three remarkably high and vertical walls making up a natural dam.

Those walls appeared to be the remains of a tremendous volcanic explosion. The center wall was a sheer cliff wall. It was roughly three hundred meters high, and it was made up of white sand and pumice. Halfway to its summit, there was a protruding lump in the shape of a gigantic belly. The bands of black sand, some exceptionally long and wide and some short and narrow running up and down the face of that wall, formed a vast and impregnated zebra.

Occasionally, countless tons of sand and rock fell away from the summit of that sheer wall. The ensuing explosion resounded for kilometers around. When all those tons of sand impacted the ground, it sent waves of dust, sand, and garbage up the hill to the foot of Pepita's steep hill and gravity gladly sent everything back to the bottom of the sheer cliff wall.

It was unfortunate for the small animals that lived at the bottom of that vertical and high wall or any animals looking for food when the countless tons of sand hit the ground. But it was also a great spectacle, like the tons of ice falling away from the glaciers of South America and Antarctica to explode in the frigid seas.

In the right lower corner, where the vertical wall and the right wall fused, a giant dead tree was lying upside down and leaning on the right wall. That tree had been dragged there by the titanic force of many landslides.

Under some of the dead branches of that tree, which rested on the ground, there was a low, dark, and narrow tunnel. That narrow tunnel led to a small pond of pure and crystal-clear water which flowed down from a rocky outcrop.

That small and narrow passage, known only to the critters of the ravine, was a portal to another world—to the natural beauty of the gorge. It led to a small jungle ecosystem untouched by human hands. It boasted exuberant vegetation, rich and diverse fauna.

Considering that that jungle existed a few steps away from the city center was undeniable evidence that miracles exist. Or perhaps the plain and simple fact was that the wilderness was surrounded by abysses, dangerous cliffs, chasms, and deep and treacherous hollows. Not to mention the poisonous snakes that made it practically inaccessible.

The rocky outcrop where the water flowed down in cobweb threads was clothed in a luxuriant garb of entangled greenery. It was embellished with tiny crimson flowers that grew interweaved with the mint hue vines' leaves that flowed down in cascades from the summit to the waters of the small pond.

The small pond was at the bottom of that massive rocky outcrop, on which Castor-oil plants grew in a significant number on the face and summit. Their branches and their broad leaves blocked most of the sun's rays, refraining them from getting to the small pond. Those rays that managed to get through the foliage came down as light green and some as diffused white rays.

The few white sun rays that shined on a narrow gold vein that ran down from the top to the bottom of the rocky outcrop gave that golden band the enchanting power to turn to gold everything its reflection touched.

All that sumptuous magnificence got reflected on the small pond mirror, turning the rocky outcrop into a shrine erected there by the hands of Mother Earth with the help of her chlorophyll children.

The small pond was not so deep, and it only reached halfway to one's knees; nonetheless, life vibrated in it, and it was home to frogs and crabs, big belly fish, turtles, water beetles, and water lilies.

The small pond gently spilled into a tunnel of wild plants and flowers and came to stop in a deep pond whose bottom was scattered with gold nuggets.

Like the small pond, the big pond had abundant aquatic life, which served as food to the day and night hunters.

The big pond's water also spilled over, and the land's inclined surface guided it like a docile lamb to the edge of a chasm, where it was compelled to jump.

As the pond's water hit the bottom, it joined the violent waters of a raging river that rushed to its rendezvous with the Caribbean Sea like a runaway wild horse.

A fair amount of ground and rocks went crashing down to the river below every rainy season, which meant the days of that beautiful lush green patch of a jungle were numbered.

But that did not ruffle the feathers of its inhabitants, especially the flocks of parrots and parakeets whose members were forever arguing and fighting over tidbits or a favorite spot.

Pepita quenched her thirst with the refreshing water of the small pond and assuaged her hunger with the meat of a couple of crabs, and with the whitish flesh of some frogs she caught. She then wallowed in the water, taking a deserved little rest.

The throbbing pain Pepita felt in her teats full of milk told her it was time to begin the long trek to her lair. Pepita arrived at the cave and as soon as she picked up the unpleasant smell that had taken Lucky away, the hair on her back stood up.

She jumped into the cave with her fangs unsheathed, ready to sink them into the bone of whatever was there. But all she found in there were two of her puppies leaning against one of the walls and shaking uncontrollably. Enraged she turned around, came out of the cave, and in a few bounds came out of the ravine. She was sniffing, listening, and looking everywhere, but sadly she found no traces or footprints, nor the stench she was following. The city's buses, like carrier vessels belching out stinking clouds of diesel black smoke, had saturated the air. Pepita tried not to pay attention to her teats throbbing pain, nor to her disabled sense of smell, and continued looking for her puppies, until she could no longer take the pain that consumed her. Pepita ceased her search and rapidly went to her lair, where the two puppies, trembling and famished, swiftly relieved her throbbing pain.

Peregrino and Mona were the only ones left of her six puppies. So, she resolved that nothing and nobody would take those two away from her. As soon as she finished feeding her babies, she picked up Peregrino by the scruff of his neck and headed down to the jungle. When Pepita got there, she left Peregrino by the side of the small pond and went looking for a new lair.

Fortunately for Pepita, she did not have to look for long, nor go far. Right away, she found a warm and pleasant place between some bushes growing under a couple of luxuriant trees. That place had a fluffy cushion of dry leaves and old man's moss.

Pepita could not believe her luck. To ensure that it did not belong to a dangerous animal, she sniffed around but found no scent or signs that it belonged to any animal. She assumed that the owner abandoned it. She went to get Peregrino and introduced him to his new den, which he liked very much. Peregrino found the seed of one of the luxuriant trees, which was so incredibly big and round that it looked like the wheel of a huge toy fire truck. Pepita felt sure nothing wrong could happen to Peregrino, so she left him playing with the enormous seed and went to get Mona.

Pepita had decided to finish raising those two babies in that magnificent green oasis, away from the reach of that penetrating stench that had taken four of her pups.

The misfortune of some could be the fortune of others. The tragedy of Peregrino's siblings was his fortune. Because now he had more than two teats full of milk just for him and in much less time than harmful pests multiply in the open sky dumps, he gained weight and grew and in a short time became chubbier and taller than

Mona. Pepita and her puppies never suffered food scarcity. She hunted and fished and collected pigeon's eggs and the eggs of other birds that build their nests in the hollow of the tree's trunks and of those on the cushion of the dead leaves on the ground as well. Pepita always complemented her puppies' diet with the scraps of food she constantly found in the dump, including the warm contents of the disposable diapers that abounded in the landfill.

GUAPO AND THE HUMONGOUS BOULDER

———————◆———————

The inexorable march of time waits for no one. The day came when Pepita weaned her pups, but for some strange reason, Pepita did not wean them when she should have, nor did she abandon them as is always done by street dogs. No, she stayed with them an exceptionally long time, pampering them, looking after them, teaching them to fish and hunt. She also took them to the dump, where she instructed them in the fine art of searching for scraps and they also learned to appreciate the great variety of dishes they could enjoy there.

Pepita felt a great love for her pups, perhaps because those two and the four abducted were her first and she never got over the fear of losing those two. Possibly that was the reason that even though they had grown bigger than her, she waited on them hand and foot as if they were little puppies.

On a beautiful, sunny day, Pepita decided to take her kids to tour the surrounding area at the top of the ravine.

When they were passing by the cave where they took their first steps, they went inside. Mona and Peregrino smelled the walls and their old toys and that brought them reminiscences of their babyhood.

Peregrino and Mona were overcome with acute nostalgia for the days of fun and games with their siblings. They remembered their names, and without realizing it, said their names out loud—Lucky, Niño, Cinderella, and Ronaldinho.

Peregrino remembered Lucky and Niño with love. Niño was the only one that understood him and the only one that shared his grief when Lucky was taken away by the monster.

Mona and Peregrino played for a short while with their old toys. When Pepita went out of the cave, they followed her to the top of the ravine. There she showed them the surroundings and then led them on a path that went all around the edge of the vast gorge.

At the end of the long walk, they ran into a massive boulder that obstructed the way. To continue their walk, they climbed the humongous boulder. It was easy for them thanks to an altruistic soul who, with hammer and chisel in hand, carved the rock to form a stairway, so anyone could use the boulder as a lookout.

That gigantic rock was twice as long, wide, and high as a Greyhound bus. Half of that rock was embedded in the ground; the other half was hanging in the air over a vertical and incredibly deep chasm. That humongous rock was there waiting for the slightest opportunity to escape from the ground's grip.

The rock wanted to escape from the ground's embrace and was there impatiently waiting for the ground to let it go away and be free to fall to the bottom. It desired to thunderously announce its freedom and it's urge to find a new love and if anyone was on top of it when its time to go came, it would gladly give them a ride.

Pepita, Peregrino, and Mona admired the majesty of the immense ravine. From the lookout, it appeared to be an ancient volcanic crater. Suddenly, Pepita felt the rock shake under her paws. She wanted to run, but her legs did not obey her. From the depths of her being, a second tremor ran through her, shaking her violently and leaving her dazed and on wobbly legs.

Mona and Peregrino were perplexed, gaping, and unable to understand what was happening to Pepita, so they just stood there, looking at her. When a new tremor shook Pepita, she knew what was happening to her.

Pepita's biological alarm was blaring. Waking in her the urge to find a male dog, Pepita climbed down to the lowest side of the rock and jumped from there to the ground, followed closely by Mona and Peregrino, who were no longer puppies, and noticed a change and a new scent in her.

When the trio of dogs reached the end of the path they were following, they found themselves face to face with the terrifying highway.

Pepita approached her children and hugged and kissed them tenderly and lovingly nibbled their ears while fanning her tail very softly. This was her subtle way of saying goodbye, and she hoped they would understand. Pepita did what she should have done when she weaned them and left them standing in front of the highway.

When Pepita saw that Mona and Peregrino stood there gaping at the highway and the vehicles speeding by, she quickly went to position herself at the edge of the asphalt ribbon. When she was sure that they were observing her, she looked at both sides of the road, waiting for the auspicious moment to cross to the other side.

Peregrino and Mona, extremely nervous, were observing her and at the same time they were emitting high-pitched squeals.

Suddenly, Pepita went out like a bullet, crossing the six lanes of death and reaching the other side alive and without a scratch. Once there, she repeated the process and got back unharmed where Mona and Peregrino were barking and yelping nervously.

When she went to kiss them, they hugged and kissed her while standing on their hind legs. As they did that, she felt the anxiety and fear that made their bodies shake uncontrollably. She hugged and kissed them one last time and went to position herself at the edge of the asphalt once more. When she saw her chance, she swiftly traversed the six lanes of the highway.

When Pepita reached the other side, she took an old and dusty earthen path and vanished around a bend in it. She did not turn around to give one last glance to those that, just a minute earlier, were her adored puppies.

Mona and Peregrino, barking and crying, heartbroken, saw Pepita disappear in the distance. Mona, grief-stricken and unable to handle the separation, was overcome with desperation. She ran to the edge of the asphalt belt. There she emulated Pepita's moves and readied herself to run across the highway.

At once, Peregrino was seized by a panic attack. Barking like a mad dog, he called Mona, while scratching the rocky ground so hard that his front paws bled.

Mona went out flying toward the other side of the road with her muscles as tense as the strings of a finely tuned guitar and her eyes on the swiftly moving vehicles. At that precise moment, Guapo, the handsome devil of the highway, materialized next to her.

Guapo was what the crossing's survivors had named that extraordinary looking dog, and death's crossing was what they named that highway. Mona gave Guapo a sideways glance, and at that instant, the world seemed to stop for her or at least go in slow motion.

In an exceptionally exotic, sexy voice, Guapo said to Mona: "Everything will be okay, baby." His voice sounded as if out of a strange and inexplicable dream. Taking Mona by her front paws, he gently pulled her close to his chest and in perfect synchronization while standing on their rear legs, they waltzed the Blue Danube of Johann Strauss as they crossed the highway.

The little hand of the car's speedometer that hit Mona was caressing one hundred and forty kilometers per hour. Mona went flying. Her body flipped several times before landing headfirst on top of a big ornamental rock at the side of the highway.

Mona lay still on the rock. The light of her eyes flickered and went out, and she lay there looking at the sky with blinded eyes. Peregrino did not know how he crossed the highway. As if in a dream, he found himself at his sister's side, trying to revive her.

Peregrino licked his sister's disfigured mouth, trying to put her life back in with his tongue. but all his desperate efforts were to no avail, since Mona had reached Heaven before her body reached the ornamental rock at the side of the highway.

With a smell of dead flowers permeated in his nose, he lay down close to his sister's lifeless body, hoping that she would wake up at any moment and be her old self again.

The sky, refusing to be a mute witness of that heartbreaking scene, covered its face with veils of darkening thunder clouds, and let out a wail of thunder while letting down a sea of tears in the form of heavy and intermittent rain.

Peregrino spent two days and two nights at the side of Mona's dead body. Around midday of the third day, he knew that she would never wake up. With a lump in his throat so big that it made it hard for him to breathe, he gave Mona one last, long look. Wishing he could shed a deluge of tears, Peregrino left, feeling like the most wretched, lonely dog in the world.

THE LONG MARCH AND THE NEIGHBORHOOD

———◆———

Peregrino followed the narrow and dusty path that Pepita had taken. That path took him to the streets and alleyways of a large, poor barrio. There he was amazed to see a considerable number of kids playing and screaming in great glee in the streets and alleyways.

Every step Peregrino took, he discovered something new. He was born and raised in the ravine; therefore, everything he saw surprised him, from the streets and alleyways to the music coming out of the houses, along with the delicious smells that the wind was forcing into his nose.

He smelled exotic aromas from far and near, as if those strange smells were the distant and tantalizing siren's songs.

As he turned around a corner and entered headlong into a narrow street, he almost stumbled face to face into Pepita. Pepita was going in the opposite direction. She was panting and looked exhausted and very thirsty; her tongue was hanging out and to one side of her mouth.

At the end of her tail, a long line of male dogs followed her. Some of the dogs were fighting, some snarling and biting each other. Many of the dogs were injured, and some had nasty, bleeding injuries, but that did not stop them. All of them wanted to earn the right to mate with Pepita, even if that meant losing an eye, an ear, or ending up with a broken bone.

The scent she was giving off was like a divine and bewitching fragrance for dogs, and the four winds were announcing her state of heat, calling more and more dogs crazed with sexual desire.

Everywhere Pepita and the long line of male dogs following her went, more street dogs joined them.

As if the significant number of street dogs were not enough, to the long march came dogs that ran away from home. There were also those that jumped the fences that kept them in their homes. Many of these dogs would never find their way home and were doomed to wander the city's streets forever. This was because the long march lasted for days on end and could take them several kilometers away from their homes, through a maze of streets and alleys and endless avenues.

Some of those dogs were too small or too weak to have the slightest opportunity to mate with Pepita, but that did not persuade them to go home.

When the sexual frenzy ends, most dogs are injured, disoriented, exhausted, thirsty, and hungry. The small and weak now have a chance with the female dog. But not only is the female no longer interested, but she also is dog tired, and in a bad mood. And for all the effort and the tireless persistence of those dogs, she could reward them with a nasty bite where it hurts them the most.

The frenzy finished, hunger and thirst pangs remind the dogs that they have a home. With a shaky first step begins their odyssey toward home. Some, while on their way home, cross paths with another female in heat, and not having learned anything of their previous adventure, they join the long, new march.

When Peregrino saw the sad state Pepita was in, his heart broke into a thousand pieces. Pepita cast a side glance at him and continued her erratic and relentless journey. Peregrino ran toward her but did not manage to get close. The lead dog and two other dogs broke formation to intercept him, snarling with bared teeth.

When Peregrino saw the imminent danger coming toward him, he quickly turned around and ran away, narrowly escaping the multiple rows of teeth that were snapping too close to the end of his tail.

The dogs ran after Peregrino a few meters and quickly returned to claim their place in the long line, but not before rolling in the dust and sinking their teeth into those dogs that had taken their place.

ALIVE AND KICKING

Peregrino did not stop running until he reached the end of the narrow street. That narrow street flowed like a river to the edge of a deep ravine. A broad and seemingly endless avenue separated what appeared to be an endless row of houses that ran parallel to the ravine. Peregrino descended the steep slopes of the deep ravine where he right away felt at home. He immediately undertook the search for food and water, because his gastric juices were cooking his guts as if they were a voracious fire.

When was the last time he had eaten anything? He did not remember; he had lost track of time. A couple of cheese buns were the first edible things he found. Not far from there, he found rainwater inside an old plastic container which was infested with mosquito larvae. Still, he drank it as if it were clean and pure.

Fortunately for Peregrino, he found a cardboard box full of smelly spaghetti near the rainwater, so he ate and drank, grateful that Lady Luck shined upon him.

Evening was falling, and Peregrino was having a hard time keeping his eyes open. He lay down and found himself drifting toward sleep. Before falling asleep completely, he heard the distant and plaintive howl of a lonely and sad dog.

As Peregrino listened to that mournful howl, he felt sure he had heard it ever since the very moment he arrived at the barrio. But as that howl joined the sounds, noises, and music coming out of the houses, he heard it faintly; it was indistinguishable.

The fateful last few days had left Peregrino alienated, so that sorrowful howl had not had any effect on him. But now that the quietness and stillness of the evening were beginning to reign in the barrio, he was able to hear and decipher it.

That howl informed him that the howler was in trouble and in dire need of food and water. Peregrino pricked his ears and focused them in the direction of that howl, so he could pinpoint where the howler was, with the good intention to go and look for that dog and see what he could do for him. Not able to keep his eyes open any longer, he succumbed to sleep.

Well into the night, Peregrino woke up feeling dazed and not quite aware of his surroundings. He got out of the ravine in a state of great uncertainty, feeling as if from the moment when Mona ran toward her death, to the moment he woke up in that new ravine, it had been one very long day.

Peregrino could not remember how or when that day full of painful and unpleasant experiences had started. He thought about Mona and Pepita, and if it had been possible for him to shed a sea of tears, he would have gladly done it. Very sad, and under cover of the night shadows, he went to investigate that mournful howl that was killing him.

A long walk along the edge of the ravine brought him to the back yard of a very old colonial-style house with thick adobe walls and a red tile roof.

For some inexplicable reason, that house had withstood intact the last great earthquake and an endless number of strong tremors. That was why new homes constructed of bricks faced the naked avenue at odds with the old house.

At the wooden fence that surrounded the back yard, a dog tied up to it was howling. That fence had seen better days, but the sun, the rain, and the lack of a coat of paint had left it faded and rotten.

The lonely dog continued his sad howl, unaware of the curious eyes behind the fence trying to take a good look at him through a small gap in the wall.

Peregrino stuck his nose in the fence's gap, trying to sniff the air to get some information about that dog through his scent. But the dog was too far from the opening, and the wind was not blowing in any direction, so it offered no help at all.

Just like when a lady walks by and stirs the air with her long and baggy dress and allows one to sense her fresh scent, in the same manner, from the skirts of the deep ravine, came up a wind that swirled around the old house, allowing the two dogs to catch their scent. That sent a tremor from their paws to their heads, leaving them stunned and unable to understand why their brains were offering them beautiful and tender reminiscences of their puppy days. The two dogs recognized each other, and in unison, from their mouths came the names of one another.

"Peregrino?"

"Lucky?"

"Peregrino!"

"Lucky!"

They stared at each other, unable to believe it. They howled, cried, and barked, possessed by irrepressible and indescribable happiness. That happiness made their tails wag so fast that it gave the impression that from one moment to the next, their tails would fly away from their bodies.

As soon as the attack of unadulterated happiness had diminished, Peregrino, who had become a big, strong, and brave dog, did not have to think twice to make the firm decision to take his brother out of that place.

Peregrino attacked relentlessly the gap where he had put his nose to sniff his brother. With claws and teeth, he ripped, pulled, tore, and sank his fangs into the wood.

Possessed by a fierce spirit, he charged at the fence, biting and ripping, while Lucky was jumping up and down thrilled, trying to free himself from the rope that held him to the barrier, spending the last ounce of energy left in him.

Peregrino did not cease his attack against the fence until he opened a big hole in it. He tried to get in through that hole, but only his head fit; his shoulders could not get through. He continued tearing and biting, not calling a truce until a large piece of wood gave way.

The opening on the wall was not big enough to let him get through freely, but Peregrino could not wait. With determination, seasoned with a pinch of impatience, he impetuously got through the opening, leaving tufts of hair, flesh, and blood in the sharp edges. But to Peregrino, pain had not the slightest importance that significant, incredible night. After all, his brother had been given up for dead, but he was there, alive and kicking.

When the two brothers had enough hugging and kissing, they chatted a little about the old times. But the weariness of a long day and a long night began to charge Peregrino for the energy used. He lay on his side on the bare ground and, unaware of it, fell asleep.

It was then that Lucky noticed his brother's wounds, so he took on the task to clean them and heal them, licking his brother and pulling out the long and sharp fragments embedded in Peregrino's flesh with his teeth.

A long and deep wound in his brother's belly was the last thing Lucky licked and healed. Completely out of energy, he let his head fall next to his brother's neck like in the old times. With a happy heart and full of joy, he lost consciousness.

The dome of the night sky, studded with the unreachable stars, shed tears of bright light upon the brothers. Canis Major shone in all its glory, impassive before the canine drama developing under its luminous paws.

At midmorning the next day, when Lucky opened his eyes, the tropic's sunrays were lashing the bulging waist of Mother Earth. Lucky tried several times to get up, but he could not do it.

Suddenly, a noxious tingling went through his body. Every square inch of his body hurt severely, and his nose, mouth, and throat were as dry as the sands of the Saharan desert at midday.

Lucky was dehydrated. He had been at that fence for five days. One of the little boys who grew up with him since he arrived at that house had promised to return in one hour. They had to tie him up every time they went out, or he would chew, tear, and destroy everything around the house, for the simple reason that he hated to be alone.

Lucky did not see it, and no one informed him, but he was sure that something terrible had happened to his family, mainly because his family, made up of two adults and two kids, had never left him alone for too long.

Lucky looked around for his brother, but Peregrino was nowhere to be found. Hopelessly he looked at the gap in the fence, wishing with all his heart that his brother had not abandoned him. He painfully rolled onto his back and exercised his legs, trying to relieve the pain and the nasty tingling that had taken over his body.

He managed to get rid of the tingling, then closed his eyes and just lay there still. Peregrino got into the back yard through the hole in the fence which he had enlarged a bit more so he would not injure himself again.

When he saw his brother lying on the ground with his legs up, it startled him. It reminded him of the way he found Mona, dead on top of the ornamental rock at the side of the highway.

He quickly went to sniff his brother's nose, and as soon as he licked his brother's mouth, Lucky opened his eyes. When he saw Peregrino, his heart became overwhelmed with happiness and gratitude.

Lucky tried to get up but could not do it, so he just lay there on his belly. Peregrino had brought a good quantity of food and water, and as soon as Lucky licked his mouth, he regurgitated food and water into Lucky's mouth and face. Lucky swallowed voraciously and avidly lifted the scattered food and the spilled water, not wanting to share even a particle with the dry and thirsty ground.

Lucky licked his face and mouth as far as his long tongue allowed. While he was doing that, Peregrino was chewing the rope that held his brother to the fence.

Peregrino finally succeeded in cutting the rope that held Lucky to the fence. He then grabbed the piece of string left around Lucky's neck, and with all his strength, dragged his brother to the opposite side of the fence, where there was a large, pleasant, cool shade.

Lucky, immensely grateful for his brother, closed his eyes. The moment he opened his eyes again, he saw Peregrino coming back from the dump with more water and food.

Lucky had lost track of time. However, knowing that his brother was taking care of him brought cheer to his heart, and that gave him the certainty that everything was going to be all right.

Peregrino once more regurgitated food and water and dropped it in Lucky's mouth. As soon as he saw that Lucky had swallowed the whole thing, he took on the task of enlarging the gap on the fence some more, so his brother could effortlessly go through it.

His task finished, Peregrino looked at the big hole he had opened and was completely satisfied. He went to see if everything was all right with Lucky and when he saw that his brother was sleeping peacefully, he went to the dump for more food and water.

ARES AND COPERNICUS

---◆◆◆---

Peregrino arrived at the dump, which already felt like home to him since it provided him with lots of food and water. But luck was disobliging that time. After a long and unsuccessful search, he got out and walked by the edge of the ravine until he found another garbage dump.

The slopes on that ravine were dangerous, almost vertical. So deep, that even if one tried to get as far down as possible with the help of a rope, one still would not be able to see the bottom.

Knowing that hunger is a bad adviser, Peregrino descended slowly and carefully.

Following a short walk, he came to a place where countless tons of garbage had accumulated. That place was insidiously offering a place to walk, eat, or even take a nap safely.

Peregrino's sense of smell guided him directly to a plastic bag full of pork meat. For some reason it had gone bad, and the local butcher had gotten rid of it there.

Peregrino started to sink his teeth into the plastic bag to tear it open. It was then he saw a couple of dogs descending toward him. The dogs did not appear friendly. They showed him their teeth, but not because they were smiling; rather, they were snarling as a sign of hostility.

The leader of the two dogs was enormous and had a red fur coat. The other dog was a short and muscular black dog.
They did not need to ask Peregrino what was in the bag, as the smell already told them; besides, whatever was in the bag belonged to them, because Peregrino was in their territory.

As is always the case between men and dogs, no one wants to share the booty. The finder keeps it or dies trying.

The two dogs descending toward Peregrino saw fit to take advantage of the higher ground they were on and pounced on Peregrino. The big dog tried to bite Peregrino's face, but Peregrino ducked, and with incredible speed, bit off one of the big dog's ears as he flew by.

The other dog had no trouble sinking his teeth in Peregrino's left shoulder. Peregrino felt a sharp and terrible pain there. He wanted to scream in pain but instinctively knew that he would give his attacker much more courage and determination if he did.

The violent attack pushed Peregrino backward, and he landed on his back. That freed his shoulder from the black dog's teeth. The black dog flew by with his hind legs way up in the air and landed heavily on his right side.

When the black dog jumped up to continue the fight, Peregrino caught him by the neck and shook him violently, making the black dog scream in pain.

The big dog fell on his face, did a somersault, and went sliding with his hind legs high in the air on top of a bunch of cardboard boxes. With his seriously injured ear bleeding and burning as if an invisible fire was devouring it, he ran toward Peregrino with only one thing in mind—to shred Peregrino to pieces.

The big dog's legs were moving fast, but they were not taking him anywhere. He appeared to be running on a fast-moving treadmill. The countless tons of garbage that had been there waiting for the right moment to go sliding down the slope, decided that that was the moment for which they had been waiting.

Peregrino and the two dogs could do nothing to save themselves. They rode downhill on top of the garbage that was flowing down like a wide river, and it swiftly swallowed them.

Pestilence, the apocalyptic pale horseman, rode on the wings of the wind as an invisible and foul-smelling cloud of methane. It came up from under the countless tons of garbage, enveloping the barrio, its surroundings, and beyond.

The trash's avalanche gathered speed as it continued flowing downhill. When it reached a wide and long ledge which edges were bent up, giving it the appearance of a pagoda roof, the avalanche slowed down and came slowly to the edge.

The garbage fell down a deep chasm like a waterfall and went crashing loudly on a large and round pond of spring water.

Four extraordinarily high and vertical walls contained the pond. The abundant algae and the light green moss that grew around the pond to the water level gave that pond a green mint hue. That green pond was home to many waterfowl, the ducks and the geese being the most numerous.

The walls that made up that pond were full of holes, in which thousands upon thousands of countless swallows nested. Those walls were of a sandy color, and because of all the holes in them, they looked exactly like old computer punch cards.

In the days of old computers, the electric company sent its trucks to dump the thousands of used-up punch cards to the deep and dangerous ravines surrounding the barrio, turning the kids of those poor neighborhoods into great artisans.

The kids used to fold and shape those cards into loops and then link them to make hats, belts, vests, and even backpacks to carry their books to school.

The green pond's waters drained out through a rocky alley and fell into a waterfall fifty meters further ahead. A couple of tributaries joined it, and it became a narrow, deep, fast-moving river that went meandering toward the northwest.

The three dogs swam the pond looking for a way out. The three had survived the avalanche and the fall, but at a high cost. The three of them had bruises, fractured ribs, and deep cuts.

The big dog had twisted one of his legs. The short black dog had one of his eyes closed and swollen, and the tip of his tail had skin and hair missing.

Floating along the river for a good stretch, Peregrino and the two dogs found themselves in a moorland of rolling dunes surrounded by the ravine's sheer walls. The river became broad and shallow, making it possible for the dogs to walk to the riverbank.

As the dogs got out of the water and walked on terra firma, they realized how severe their injuries were. Their bodies turned heavy, and the pain became unbearable.

Since they found the ground too hard to walk on, they returned to the shallow, muddy, warm water, which lightened their weight, soothed their pain, and healed their wounds.

The painful adventure that almost cost the dogs their lives, united them with brotherly ties. They licked one another's wounds and cuts in the muddy, shallow water as if they were old friends.

Peregrino said his name and he immediately began telling his life's story. He finished by saying he was afraid he would not see his brother again, because it was impossible to climb up the sheer walls surrounding the moorland. And if that was not bad enough, he said, "I'm utterly lost with no idea where I am right now."

"You are in the water," said the short black dog, trying to be funny. The three dogs looked at each other and were it not for the pain in their muscles and in their every bone and even every hair in their bodies, they would have laughed out loud. So, they gulped down the laughter to enjoy it some other time.

"My name is Copernicus, but all my friends call me Nikus," said the short black dog. "I came from Italy with my human family, but I escaped from them to explore this new world."

"Mine is Ares, due to the color of my fur. I'm pure Guatemalan, and I like to dance the Guatemalan jig," said the big dog proudly.

When all their names were stated, and the new friends had a little chat that only dogs find interesting, Ares and Nikus told Peregrino that not only did they know Lucky, but they also knew where to find him.

"Don't worry," said Nikus. "As soon as we find a way to get back to the barrio, we will take you to your brother."

Ares and Nikus also told Peregrino that they slept in the hollow of a large tree standing by the ravine's edge where they had attacked him. "Nothing personal," said Ares. "But you understand that that is our territory; you would have done the same! Wouldn't you?" Peregrino nodded in agreement.

Ares went on to tell their newfound friend that one night they heard his brother howling for a long time. So, they went to see what was wrong with him. Seeing that there was nothing they could do, they left him to his fate. "After all," said Nikus, "no dog in his right mind would forcefully enter, break into, and tear a human lair to free a fellow dog."

What he had done for his brother, concurred the two dogs, was the sum of love and courage, and they let him know that they admired and respected him for it.

Ares and Nikus also apologized for the pain and the unpleasantness they caused him, blaming it on their violent nature and selfishness.

"You do not have
"After all, if it were n
perhaps we wouldn't hav

"It was no one's fault,"
la forza del destino."

Weariness, hunger, and
eyes. Nonetheless, the need
felt was killing them. Per   newfound
friends managed to sleep in the shallow, warm water,
placing their heads on each other's shoulders.

As soon as Peregrino closed his eyes, he found himself sliding downward on top of the avalanche of garbage. Suddenly, invisible claws dragged him under the river of waste. A newspaper page covered his face, keeping him from breathing.

When the avalanche reached the broad and long ledge that looked like the roof of a pagoda, he managed to get his head out of the garbage, opened his mouth wide, and breathed so frantically that his throat loudly whistled. When he reached the edge of the ledge and saw the deep chasm's large green eye looking at him, his own eyes nearly came out of their cavities as he fell to the green pond.

One-thousandth of a second before hitting the water, Peregrino woke up startled. For a second, he felt sure he still was sliding in the darkness under the avalanche of garbage, because everything was completely dark. He could not see anything, not even his newfound friends who were sleeping tightly, huddled near him.

When Peregrino looked up at the sky, the stars let him know it was well into the night. When his eyes got used

...d see his surroundings and his new

...discovered that the sounds he heard in his ...hich sounded astoundingly like the musical ...he extraterrestials played to communicate with the ...thlings in the movie, close encounters of the third kind, were nothing more than his stomach complaints and those of his friends.

Peregrino was hungry. He was so hungry, that the large parasites in his stomach were cannibalizing the small ones. Peregrino got out of the water and tried finding something to eat.

Slowly and painfully, he got up, his new friends half-asleep, found each other's shoulders, and settled down to continue sleeping.

He got out of the water quietly and following the riverbank, came to a large puddle full of frogs and crabs. Immediately he remembered Pepita's advice when she taught him to fish.

"If you want to eat more than one crab," she had said, "no matter how hungry you are, never eat the first one you catch. Crush it and go for the next and the next one after that."

Following Pepita's advice helped Peregrino catch a sizable number of frogs and crabs.

It was easy pickings for Peregrino since he surprised them while mating and romance turned into panic.

The lovers ran to the ravine's wall where there was no way out, instead of running or, in the case of the frogs, leaping into the river where they would have escaped easily.

When he finished gathering in one spot the frogs and crabs he had caught, he howled and barked loudly, calling his new friends. His friends barked and howled back, and quicker than it takes a mosquito of the garbage dump to suck the blood out of a person and leave in their bloodstream a virus, his new friends were by his side.

Ares and Nikus had never eaten that kind of food before. But as hungry as they were, they did not think that was the right time to pretend to be sophisticated diners, connoisseurs of haute cuisine. So, they ate the crunchy crabs and the cold, rubbery frogs with gusto.

When the last little crab leg went finely grounded down Nikus' gullet, he said he was still starving.

"So am I," said Ares.

"That is great!" exclaimed Peregrino. "That assures us that you are a couple of young, strong, and healthy canines. The bad news is that we are out of food and what we ate was only to stay alive, not to fatten ourselves. But if you are hungry," he said, pointing with his nose, "there is the puddle full of frog's eggs."

Ares and Nikus tried the frothy eggs, but they found the slimy eggs did not agree with their taste buds. They got out of the puddle, grimacing and spitting. Ares, seized by a body tremor, shook and vomited. When the shaking subsided, he stood there half dazed and looking down at what he had regurgitated, while slimy drool hung from his half-opened mouth.

Nikus, worried for his friend's well-being, came to his side and said, "Are you okay, Ares?' Not waiting for an answer from his friend, he asked him while pointing with his nose to Ares' vomit, "Are you going to eat that?"

Ares glowered at Nikus in a very reproachful way for his lack of good manners and said, "You know I am." Then, he swallowed what he had vomited in a single gulp.

Peregrino mockingly asked his friends, "How were the eggs, boys?"

Ares replied with a snappy answer. It was the kind of answer some dogs wish they could have given to a particular sort of dog at the right time, but they only think of it when they have already missed their chance. "Delicious, they tasted like a blueberry milkshake with a touch of lemon."

"Yeah, right," said Peregrino as he turned around and guided his friends along the riverbank.

They had not walked far when they came to a stream of nice warm water. They accepted the stream's invitation and got in the water, and immediately it caressed their wounds and soothed their pain.

The three friends walked against the gentle current with the water up to their chests, except Nikus, whose head was the only part of his body not wet. After a short walk in the warm water, they reached the entrance to a cavern with a large and high ceiling. They went in, and when they found a shallow and sandy spot, they settled down to sleep in the same way they had done in the river.

THE GERMANS

Morning rose to ducks quacking, geese honking, and birds singing. The dogs were feeling much better about their wounds and bruises and came out of the cave to greet the new day. They discovered the moorland to be teeming with wildlife and they became happy to be alive. The three amigos were amazed at the miraculous show of Mother Nature developing right in front of their eyes.

Hundreds of ducks and geese were flying low, patrolling the river as far as the eye could see and making a tremendous racket, loud enough to wake the dead.

Over the heads of ducks and geese occupying all the air space available, thousands upon thousands of swallows were flying like bullets in all directions, turning the moorland and its steep slopes into a wide, black and white, rapidly moving river.

Three hundred meters up in the sky, circling like a twister, were hundreds of black vultures soaring effortlessly, taking advantage of the updrafts. They had come to investigate the previous day's foul smell release by the avalanche of garbage.

The dogs stood there a long while admiring the natural beauty of the ravine, looking everywhere, at everything, for that place was beautiful enough to gladden anyone's heart.

A sizable number of nests were scattered around the riverbanks. The abundant reeds water lilies, and the cattails were making their best effort to choke the river, which at that spot became narrower and made a sudden turn to the right and disappeared behind the undulating field.

A warm and fickle wind was combing the tall flowering grasses in whimsical styles. The light brown tall reeds' flowers, like a soft brown rug, covered the steep walls of the ravine and the small dunes. The small dunes, like waves of a stormy sea, appeared to be rolling away from the moorland, widening the landscape and giving it a finishing touch Vincent van Gogh style.

Peregrino and his friends began the day's activities gathering eggs of all sizes and colors for breakfast. They didn't care a hoot about the squawking and protests of the owners.

There were duck eggs, geese eggs, and all kinds of waterfowl eggs, local and foreign, including Canadian geese.

The boys found a smooth, flat rock near the river's edge and decided to use it as a makeshift table for breakfast. They placed all their eggs there. When they were ready to sit down at the table, Peregrino saw something that grabbed his attention. He jumped into the water and dragged to shore the plastic bag full of meat, the same bag the now friends had fought over the previous day.

Ares and Nikus helped Peregrino drag the bag to the makeshift table. There they tore it open with their teeth and got out of it a good quantity of pork meat that was mainly bacon. That time, Mother Nature and Lady Luck provided them with bacon and eggs for breakfast.

The friends ate their fill, and when they could eat no more, Peregrino and his friends walked slowly and lazily to reach the thermal springs. There they rested their heads on the sand out of the water and slumbered for about three hours, while the warm water took care of their wounds.

The barking of some dogs approaching awakened the friends and put them on red alert. Immediately they stood on their hind legs, trying to see who it was. But whoever they were, the dunes and the tall grass concealed them completely.

They could not see the dogs, but they knew those dogs were coming their way. The three friends focused their ears in the direction of the barking, and as they attentively listened, they learned that it was six dogs. The sound of their barking told them that those dogs coming their way were not ordinary dogs; they were big, mean, and trained by man.

"Foreigners!" exclaimed Nikus with great alarm in his voice.

"Germans for sure," said Ares while looking at Peregrino expectantly.

"We are not physically fit to face that kind of canine, let alone two against one," said Peregrino. That said, a violent seizure grabbed hold of him. When the sudden episode subsided, Peregrino, unaware of why or how, recited: "Make haste lest thou shall perish!" Those enigmatic words came out hoarsely while his eyes rolled up, and Ares and Nikus could only see the whites of them. That sent shivers down their spines and from there to the rest of their bodies.

Immediately after he came out of that short and mysterious episode, Peregrino took off like a cannonball in the direction of the cavern, which was roughly fifty meters away.

When he reached the cavern entrance, he jumped out of the water. Instead of getting into the cave to hide, Peregrino quickly swerved to the left and went as fast as his legs could take him along the ravine wall that ran parallel to the river. When he came to a clearing in the undergrowth and trees, where he could see the plastic bag, which still had lots of pork meat in it, he ran in that direction.

"It is not the right moment to be thinking about food," said Ares, who was running at Peregrino's side. Peregrino did not bother to answer him and went running by the plastic bag and jumped in the river, where swimming with quick short strokes did not take him long to reach the opposite side, followed closely by Ares and Nikus.

Once out of the water, Peregrino followed the riverbank to one of the dunes that was under a luxuriant tree. That dune had an excellent view of the thermal waters, the cavern entrance, and a clear view of the whole area across the river.

Nikus was the last one to get under the tree. He lay down to the right of Peregrino and closed his eyes. Suddenly, six German shepherds appeared out of the bushes and the tall grass, right at the spot where the three friends had been resting.

Behind the dogs came ten men armed to the teeth. All of them carried AK-47s, the favorite of the drug traffickers.

When the German shepherds arrived at the spot where the friends had been resting, they picked up the three amigos' scent. And in that instant, the gates of Hell opened with vehemence. The six dogs exploded in tremendous barks of alarm and fanned out as if regurgitated from the very depths of Hell. Like rabid dogs barking and running in all directions, the German shepherds went looking for the intruders with only one thing in mind, to tear them apart. The drug traffickers were alarmed, they dropped to the ground, and immediately sent red hot metal in all directions.

Many projectiles went by whistling too close to the three friends' heads and others too close to their legs. The explosions' intense noise, whistles, whip cracks, and the *click, click, click* of the tremendous gunfire sent ducks, geese, swallows, foxes, rabbits, and anything that could swim, run, fly, hop, or crawl at top speed in the direction of the green pond.

The gunfire's echo followed the fleeing animals and went to die at the perforated walls of the green pond as suddenly as it was born out of metal and fire.

The bullet that hit Peregrino's back went in and out, not touching any essential parts. As it went out of Peregrino, it passed by, caressing Nikus' head hair and finally burying itself in the three. Peregrino did not feel the bullet's impact, nor any pain. When Peregrino turned his head to one side to protect his eyes from the dirt and stones that were flying to his face every time the bullets impacted the ground in front of him, he saw blood on Nikus' face.

"Nikus! They shot you!" Peregrino exclaimed.

Nikus, who had his eyes closed, opened them. He looked scared, and when he saw blood in one of his front legs, he cried, "I'm dying! I'm dying!" Then, with a weak voice and languid eyes like those of a dying man, he looked at Ares, and in a faltering voice said, "Ares, only you know where I bury my bones. Give them to those most in need." Those words said, he fainted.

When the drug traffickers reloaded their weapons for the second time, they got up, aiming their guns in all directions, and fired a few more shots for good measure. Once convinced that they were not in any danger, they walked toward the cavern entrance.

When Nikus regained consciousness, he saw his friends licking his face. "What happened?" he asked, almost crying. "Am I in the arms of the Lord? Am I in the kingdom of heaven?"

"No, you are okay, they did not shoot you," said Ares.

"They did not hit me. Whose blood is that then?" The two friends looked at Peregrino simultaneously.

"Oh no! Peregrino, they shot you!" exclaimed Ares. "Please, Peregrino, do not die on me!" begged Nikus, choked up.

"Who me? No, not me; I don't even feel any pain."

"He sure is brave, is he not, Ares?"

"He sure is," responded Ares, and immediately they began to lick Peregrino's wound till it stopped bleeding. By the time the smoke cleared, and peace and tranquility returned to the canyon, there were many dead birds, some in their nests, others floating in the river.

Two of the German shepherds were bullet riddled. The four dogs left, combed the whole area, till they came to the flat rock with the plastic bag on it. They sniffed the bag and turned their faces the other way disdainfully. The three friends who had been watching the German shepherds looked at each other with disbelieving facial expressions. "What!" exclaimed Ares, surprised. "Germans do not eat pork?" What the three amigos didn't know was that those dogs owners trained them exceptionally well. Leftovers and garbage were not part of their diet. No, they ate ground beef mixed with olive oil twice a day.

The German shepherds followed the friends' tracks to the riverbank and were about to get in the water to continue the search on the other side when they heard a whistle. They stopped dead in their tracks, because they knew their masters were calling them and immediately ran to join them.

Not able to continue looking for the intruders upset the German shepherds. But like the good soldiers they were, they did not make their own decisions. They obeyed, and as they say, no brain no pain, as soon as their masters sent them into the cavern, they forgot about the intruders.

One of the drug traffickers stayed outside the cavern, while another crouched down at the cave's entrance lighting the way with a powerful flashlight. The rest of the men went into the cavern following the dogs.

Two hours later, a man and a woman wearing shorts, bulletproof vests, and caressing an AK-47 each, came out of the cavern.

The man and the woman greeted the men who had remained outside of the cavern. The man wearing shorts lit up an extra-large and extra-thick Marijuana cigar. When they finished smoking, the woman sent a loud whistle toward the cavern entrance. Not long after that whistle, the four German shepherds came out, followed by the men who had gone inside the cavern. Seven men came out carrying a large and heavy burlap bag each, and the eighth man was carrying a pickaxe and a shovel.

When they finished burying the two dead dogs, the drug traffickers lit a mega large and mega thick Marijuana cigar and chatted and smoked for a spell. When the last particle of cannabis was inhaled, the caveman and his cavewoman disappeared in the darkness of the cavern. Peregrino and his friends had not missed the action that went on along the other side of the river. When the drug traffickers took the trail that would lead them back to where they had come from, they saw their chance to get out of the moorland.

As the men and the dogs disappeared behind the first dune, Peregrino and company swam soundlessly to the other side of the river. Keeping a reasonable distance, their eyes wide open and their sense of smell finely tuned, they followed the drug traffickers' tracks.

THE ENLIGHTENED CANINE

———◆———

Peregrino and friends followed the drug traffickers and their dogs for what seemed a long time. Suddenly, they heard the barking of the German shepherds followed by gunshots. The three friends climbed a large boulder to the right of the trail to see ahead of the path.

From the boulder's top, the dogs saw that the trail ended at the foot of an earthwork roughly two hundred meters farther ahead. On this embankment were parked four shiny, brand-new, four-wheel-drive vehicles.

The earthwork was at the foot of an artificial, steep ramp, narrow and dangerous, forming an angle of roughly fifty degrees with the embankment.

Three of the vehicles on the earthwork were black, and their windows tinted. Those three cars were big and intimidating. The fourth vehicle was a white police car with lettering on its sides that said Guatemala City Police. Under that lettering, it said in Latin, "Semper Fidelis."

Four men, one of them in police uniform, had gotten out of one of the vehicles and walked to rendezvous with their accomplices.

Once all of the men were at the embankment, they placed the heavy burlap bags inside the vehicles. That done, they got in the cars, including the German shepherds, and began to climb up the dangerously steep slope.

That steep incline had stones of all shapes and sizes strewn all over, and it was full of deep and narrow crevices caused by rain and wind. That ramp was neglected on purpose to ward off the curious.

Knowing the danger of that incline, the drug traffickers climbed very carefully, not wanting to lose their lives or their precious cargo.

After a little bit of rock and roll and small jumps, they reached the top of the ramp. Two of the vehicles disappeared in the first alley of the barrio; the others disappeared in the distance.

With Peregrino leading the way, the three amigos had no trouble climbing the steep ramp. When they reached the top of it, Peregrino adopted a fast and cheerful pace. Ares and Nikus had to speed up to catch up with him.

Happy to have come to no harm during his most recent adventure, Peregrino excitedly thought he would soon see Lucky. That thought gave him the certainty that, if he followed the edge of the ravine, it would take him directly to the place where he left his dear brother.

When Ares and Nikus finally caught up with Peregrino, he, without turning around to see them, said, "What happened to you boys? Did you get lost?"

"If my memory serves me correctly, which it does, you had said that you did not know the barrio," said Ares.

Before Peregrino could answer, Nikus spoke to Ares, but he really was speaking to Peregrino, or as they say in the barrio, "Say it to Peter so Paul can hear."

Nikus said, "You know, Ares, I think it is truthfully very little what our friend here doesn't know. Thoughts, ideas, knowledge, and understanding comes naturally and fluidly to him. He is pure-hearted, brave, and enigmatic. I'm sure he is an enlightened canine."

"A what?" asked Peregrino.

"Enlightened," said Ares.

"And that is what?" asked Peregrino.

"According to the legend, an enlightened canine is someone extraordinary with the power of knowledge, who is born among us canines every fifty years."

"Fifty years!" exclaimed Peregrino. "But who among us can live that long to know that? Mainly with Guapo at large."

"Guapo!" exclaimed Ares. "I didn't know you knew about Guapo. Have you seen him?"

"Obviously!" answered Nikus, taking the words right out of Peregrino's mouth. "What did I tell you? He is an enlightened canine," said Nikus triumphantly.

Ares chose to ignore Nikus' interruption and continued saying, "Rumor has it that the legend was born with Guapo. He was an enlightened canine and now hates the canine species because of a betrayal by his best friend."

"Who was an enlightened canine, right?" said Peregrino, taking the words right out of Ares' mouth.

"See! what did I tell you?" said Nikus to Ares, genuinely happy to have discovered an enlightened canine in Peregrino. So, he continued saying, "Not only is he an enlightened canine, but our friend here is a war hero wounded in action. Besides all that, did you see all the crabs and frogs he caught to feed us? I haven't the slightest idea of how he did that in total darkness."

"That is right!" said Ares. "I could not have done that even in broad daylight, even if I had to feed my mother."

"You don't have a mother," Nikus reminded Ares.

Ares glared at Nikus and was about to say something nasty, but changed his mind and continued saying, "What about the trick he played on the Germans and their masters, eh? He knew how to watch them without being seen and then followed them to find the trail that got us out of the moorland."

"That is right!" said Nikus. "Peregrino," he said solemnly in Italian. "Amico tu sei un illuminato. My friend, you are an enlightened one."

"Listen, guys, it wasn't a big deal; I thought of it first, that's all. Besides, if I was an enlightened one, and I am not saying I am, but if I was, don't you think I could come up with some inspiring and poetic words to complement our adventure? Or at least come up with some beautiful words to go with that beautiful sunset?"

As the three of them looked at the horizon, Peregrino said, "All I can think of is to tell you to walk proudly with your tail up, so the sun god's last rays of light can kiss the rear entrance to your innards."

"Inspiring and poetic enough, right, Ares?" asked Nikus.

"Amen!" said Ares.

The three amigos lifted their tails, and feeling proud of their accomplishment, adopted a cheerful and accelerated trot. The horizon was smothering the last rays of solar light, and as they gently ebbed away, capriciously turned the cumulus clouds near the horizon into soft pink cotton candy.

MARÍA MARGARITA

It was night when the boys arrived at the hollow trunk of a large and leafy tree that served as Ares' and Nikus' lair. They were tired, thirsty, and hungry, so they wasted no time and went straight to where they always found lots of food and water: María Margarita's home.

The barrio's dogs knew María Margarita and all of them knew the way to her house. Even some dogs from faraway places came to visit her.

María Margarita's home, by some strange coincidence, was called by her neighbors and dogs alike, the Halfway to Heaven Hotel.

María Margarita knew all the barrio's dogs and beyond. It was well known by all the dogs, that if a dog was injured, sick, hungry, thirsty, or needed a place to stay for a few days, the Halfway to Heaven Hotel was always there.

It was always open, any time of day or night; whether María Margarita was at home or not, dogs were always welcome. As a result, there were always dogs at the hotel, sometimes up to twenty at the same time. Many of them went there when they were hungry, and others went there because of sickness, wounds, or broken bones. But none of the dogs ever overstayed their welcome.

María Margarita had an innate knowledge of a dog's anatomy, as well as knowledge of their sicknesses. With only herbs, olive oil, garlic, and lemon, she could perform miracles and raise the dying from among the dead.

María Margarita's main door was always ajar. All a dog had to do to enter was to push it, and little bells would sound as the door opened, announcing his arrival. The dogs in charge of welcoming the visitors would come to see who it was, and they would take the visitor to wherever María Margarita was at that moment.

María Margarita usually examined new visitors. She would take them to the back yard if she did not see signs of sickness, wounds, or broken bones. There she offered them abundant food, water, and the cool shade of a leafy Ceiba tree. María Margarita always kept an eye on new visitors for signs of illness.

The dogs that went to the Halfway to Heaven Hotel looking for help got it with love and respect from María Margarita. This was a lot better than the way they treated her when she had no choice but to get help for herself in public hospitals.

Every time María Margarita went shopping or went out looking for sick or run-over dogs, the whole neighborhood enjoyed María Margarita's show. "Here comes Mary Poppins," they would say, and they would stop doing whatever they were doing to watch her.

María Margarita was a short lady whose long black hair was being devoured unkindly by gray hair that she tried to hide under a broad-brimmed hat. A long black dress covered her body. Her shoes were also black and looked like Dutch clogs, excellent for squashing cockroaches.

It was a great spectacle to see María Margarita walk, surrounded by so many dogs protecting her like the real treasure she was for them.

María Margarita had in one hand a bag full of doggy treats for those dogs she encountered on her way. In her other hand, she had the ropes with which she pulled a carpeted dolly, which she used as an ambulance to carry those dogs that were too sick or too injured to walk.

María Margarita always greeted her neighbors in a friendly manner, but never stopped to chat with anyone. She was the kind of person who, the more people she knew, the more she loved dogs.

As the procession progressed, more dogs came to join the parade. Some of them only came to kiss her hands and as soon as they obtained their treat, they moved away submissively; in the same way, some people fortunate enough to approach the Pope to kiss his hand and receive their benediction move out of the way.

Many dogs joined the parade to enjoy the street party, where no dog dared show its fangs threateningly to fellow canines.

When Ares and Nikus pushed open María Margarita's door to get in the house, Peregrino stayed outside. Never had he entered a home in his life before, and he was not going to start now.

The moment Peregrino saw the dogs that came to welcome his friends, he did not know what to do. This was perfectly understandable since he knew nothing of the golden rule of the Halfway to Heaven Hotel.

The golden rule, which all of the barrio's dogs knew and respected with all their hearts, went something like this: "No dog shall get into any fight. No dog shall incite others to fight. No dog shall partake in any violence in this house or its surroundings or suffer the consequences."

When Peregrino was ready to leave, Ares and Nikus came out of the house. Ares held the door open while Nikus tried to convince Peregrino to get in the place.

"Come on, Peregrino, get in, everything will be alright," shouted Ares from the door.

Peregrino hesitantly approached the entrance, and Nikus said, "Come on," and pushed him in with all his might while saying, "Everything will be okay; we are all friends here."

Once inside the house, Peregrino was surrounded by eight dogs. As they sniffed him, they could feel that he was in fear and anxiety's grasp.

"Everything is okay," Nikus said as the eight dogs pushed Peregrino to where María Margarita was sitting. She was reading her favorite book in her favorite recliner, which had seen better days like the rest of the furniture.

The dogs pushed Peregrino directly into María Margarita's hands. Peregrino had never had a close encounter with humans before. He had seen them walk by at the edge of his ravine and saw them when he arrived at the barrio looking for Pepita, but this was new and different.

He wanted to escape, but some fifteen dogs surrounded him, and they all were staring directly at his eyes, so he dared not move or even blink. "What have we here?" said María Margarita with a voice so gentle, so sweet, it made him relax instantly.

Peregrino did not know what María Margarita was saying, but her voice and her caressing were hypnotizing. She caressed his face, his ears, and his belly with her incredibly soft hands. He closed his eyes and instantly found himself walking on a beautiful quiet beach, where the warm turquoise water came gently to kiss the white pebbled sands full of colorful seashells.

As far as Peregrino could see, the fronds of hundreds upon hundreds of palm trees, swaying gently in the sea breeze and looking like drunkards on parade.

Behind a high wooden fence, he saw Lucky barking, but as if something or someone had turned off the sound of the world and life, he could not hear any sound coming out of him.

"Peregrino! Peregrino!" he heard a distant voice call his name. As he opened his eyes, he saw María Margarita caressing his face and looking at him sweetly. "You are a traveler and a dreamer, so I think I will call you Peregrino. Do you like your new name?" she asked, not expecting an answer.

Peregrino did not understand what she was saying, but he loved the sound of her voice. "My name is Peregrino," he said shyly, but she did not understand a word of what he said either.

María Margarita got up from the old chair and addressed the dogs. "Boys, this is Peregrino, he is now one of us, so let all the dogs know it," she said solemnly. All the dogs there wagged their tails, welcoming him.

"Ares, Copernicus, and Peregrino," said María Margarita, and the three dogs followed her to the back yard, where she fed them abundantly. When they had eaten their fill, she made them swallow four mini sausages; each was filled with healing medicine of her own making.

She also made them swallow a good quantity of water, into which she had mixed a few drops of her healing elixir. That done, she took them hurriedly to the door where she hugged and kissed them, sending them on their way.

The three friends licked María Margarita's face and hands, which was their way of saying thank you, and they wagged their tails to say goodbye. María Margarita remained at the door, watching them leave while silently saying a prayer to Saint Lazarus, patron saint of dogs, the homeless, and the lepers.

The three amigos were walking briskly despite being tired and having their bellies about to burst. "How did she know I had the urge to get out of there?" asked Peregrino without bothering to turn his head to look at his friends. And before they could answer, he also asked, "Are all humans as sweet as she is?"

Ares and Nikus found those questions amusing and decided to answer one each. "She is an enlightened one," said Nikus.

Before Nikus could go on with his favorite topic, Ares said, "No, not all humans are like her, and some of them you should truly fear."

Peregrino stopped his brisk pace for a second, turned around, and gazed intently into his two friends' eyes as if he found it hard to believe that humans were mean enough to harm a dog.

His friends stared at him expectantly, yet Peregrino did not say a single word, nor did he make the slightest sound. Peregrino continued walking, and with the incredible urge to see his brother, he accelerated his pace a bit more, and his friends followed. Suddenly Ares and Nikus looked at each other when they simultaneously got the weird feeling that they had been following him all their lives.

THE TV EVANGELIST

———◆———

L ucky was desperate. His brother had been gone for a long time, and there were no signs of him. "Did something terrible happen to him? Did he go back to his home? If he did, why did he not come to say goodbye?"

Lucky kept asking himself those and many more questions constantly since the previous days. Anxiety and despair had taken over his mind and body and that rendered him powerless.

Lucky felt helpless before the adverse situation where he was free of the rope that held him to the fence. Nonetheless, he was still tied to that house by an invisible and unbreakable rope. For that reason, trying to go out into the world of the barrio to find his brother was a futile effort.

Lucky had come to that house when he was just a baby, and never was he allowed by his overprotective family to go out by himself, like most dogs of the neighborhood that went out to meet friends and be home for lunch.

His family was afraid he could be attacked by the street dogs that were everywhere or be run over by a vehicle. Trying to find a solution to his predicament, he paced the back yard back and forth like a caged lion.

Lucky kept sticking his head through the gap in the fence, trying to see his brother. He would stretch his neck as far as the fence would allow him. He would look left and right, but as his brother was nowhere in sight, he went back to pacing back and forth.

Every time Lucky was at the gap in the fence, he had the certainty that he could quickly jump to the other side, but every time Lucky tried, he was pulled back by the invisible and unbreakable rope that bound him to the house.

When he thought there was no way out for him, he remembered that his brother appeared during his howling, so Lucky decided to howl again. As soon as he started howling and hoping his brother would appear again, he heard a loud bark. He looked at the gap in the fence the moment his brother came in through it.

Lucky ran to kiss his brother. As soon as he licked Peregrino's mouth, his brother regurgitated the medicine and the mini sausages that María Margarita had compelled him to swallow.

Lucky dived to the ground mouth first and gulped down the food and the liquid his brother had brought for him to eat and drink. As soon as Lucky took care of what his brother had brought him, Ares and Nikus regurgitated sausages and natural medicine.

Lucky looked at his brother, unsure of what to do. Peregrino gazed straight at him and nodded. That was all Lucky needed to dive into the food, and he avidly ate the food the strangers offered him.

When Lucky finished eating, Peregrino introduced him to his friends. Ares and Nikus regurgitated their most recent adventure as if it were gastric acid because their throats and tongues were burning to tell the story. They told it with luxurious detail, and they did it the way Hollywood does with real-life stories, exaggerating here and there to make it much more thrilling.

As they were telling the story, now and then they would say, "Right, Peregrino?" to see if he agreed with that version of the story. Peregrino would nod with a great smile in his eyes as if he wasn't there to live the adventure.

Nikus was halfway into the story he was telling for the second time when he succumbed to sleep. But by then, his friends were snoring.

When they woke up the next day, the first thing Lucky did was tell Nikus to continue with the story. And he apologized for falling asleep while he was telling it. "Don't worry about it, we all fell asleep," said Nikus.

"Yesterday was an exceptionally long day for all of us, do you remember where I was in the story?"

"No," said Lucky, then he added, "would you be so kind as to start from the beginning?"

"I will be pleased to do it." When Nikus finished telling the story again, they all fell silent with big smiles in their hearts.

Peregrino got up from where he had been lying down and placed his right paw on Lucky's forehead. When he talked, he did it with thunder in his voice and his words came out of his mouth in precisely the way in which TV evangelists usually talk.

"Are you willing to change your life?" Peregrino asked his brother.

"Yes, I am!" said Lucky excitedly.

"Are you willing and able to be born again and start a new life?"

"I am," said Lucky with a shaky voice as he trembled all over.

"Can you break the ties that bind you to this house?"

"No, I can't!" he cried aloud and shuddered uncontrollably. "My body and mind are unwell, but I believe, brother, that I shall be well if you say the word."

Peregrino's physical and mental pressure on his brother was so powerful that Lucky fell to the floor in the same manner that some believers fall when their pastor touches their forehead.

"Spirit of servility! Spirit of weakness! Spirit of cowardice! Phobos and Deimos! Come out of this body, I command you!" Peregrino said it with thunder in his voice, and the tremor on Lucky's body instantly ceased.

Peregrino embraced his brother, and while trying to help him up from the ground, whispered sweet words in his ear as if he was talking to a newborn baby.

When Peregrino saw that his brother did not react to his encouragement, but remained motionless on the ground, he stood firmly on his four legs and, regaining his voice of thunder, he said, "Get up, brother Lucky! You have been freed of your chains! You have the right to take your first step out of this house. Get up and walk, I command you!"

Lucky jumped up from the ground, full of a new joyful spirit, and in a playful mood, he approached the gap on the fence and jumped out into the street. Ares and Nikus did not have the slightest idea of how out of their mouths came a loud, "Hallelujah!"

MI CASA ES TU CASA (MY HOME IS YOUR HOME)

———◆———

The four amigos spent the day having lots of fun and searching for food and water in the garbage dump of the ravine that was Ares' and Nikus' territory. They spent so much quality time with each other that they felt inseparable at the end of the day.

When that beautiful day ended, Ares and Nikus went along the ravine's edge, leading the two brothers to the tree hollow that was their lair, which was big enough to shelter the four of them.

The happiness of that great day was marred by a sense of foreboding, by a sign of something sad and painful approaching at great speed, as if a freight train was coming directly to hit them. Ares led the single file walk. Peregrino trailed behind, thoughtful and gloomy. His traveling companions turned to see him, then looked each other in the eyes, and without saying a word, they went on their way with the poisonous snake of apprehension coiled in their hearts. When they finally reached the hollow of a large tree trunk, Ares said, "Mi casa es tu casa, boys. My home is your home." Nikus felt like saying, "our home," but he had not the slightest desire to speak, so he closed his eyes and lay on the ground, as did his friends. Some of them looked at the ground and the others closed their eyes fearing the worst, fearing the inevitable. They knew that the moment Peregrino opened his mouth, it would be to tell them that they would have to say goodbye and part ways.

After a long, deafening silence, Nikus fearing the world had stopped, he got up from the spot where he was lying and gathering up all his courage, said: "I wish you would stay with us; our home is your home. We have enough food and room for all of us, and if we ever run out of food, there is always the Halfway to Heaven Hotel." Nikus' words came out weak, because of the lump in his throat, which he felt was as big as a watermelon.

Not one of his friends reacted to his words, because it was easier for a Tyrannosaurus Rex with a few hundred pounds of meat marinating in its digestive juices to pass through the eye of a needle, than their words to pass through the lump in their throat.

Nikus, feeling that their beautiful friendship was slipping away like water through their fingers, tried to make Ares come to his aid. Looking at Ares straight in the eye and gesturing with hands and shoulders Italian style, he said with powerless words, "That right, Ares?"

"That's right!" said Ares, coming out of his pensive and saddened mood.

"It would be an honor and give us great happiness if you could stay here with us. We could share many new adventures now that we know where to go duck hunting, and we could discover together what is behind those mountains and beyond the horizon."

Seeing no reaction from his friends, Ares lay down quietly.

A short silence that felt like an eternity forced Peregrino to get up and say, "Thank you, boys. Believe you me, nothing would make us happier than to be able to accept that invitation; but the two of us have a long journey ahead of us. We have many threads to rejoin, fibers cut off in our early days, and if we hope to weave our destiny, we must go, and as much as it hurts us to leave you, it is a journey we must take alone."

That said, Peregrino felt silent, and silence again reigned in the hollow of the large tree trunk. He could not explain to his friends the real reason why they could not stay, because he did not know it.

Why leave if they have excellent and real friends, plenty of food, a safe place to sleep, and the promise of many adventures? Something life does not offer as an everyday gift to man or beast. What more could a flea-ridden dog ask from life? If that was always the canine golden dream, Peregrino could not understand why they could not stay. Was he not longing to feel the hypnotic caresses of María Margarita? Nevertheless, something stronger was calling him to the two realms of his ravine. Something deeply mysterious. Something like a beam of light in the darkness attracted him, and all efforts to resist were futile. If the reasons for not staying, reasons that were shrouded in mystery for Peregrino, were not enough, a terrible feeling of guilt for not being there for Mona and Pepita when they were in danger was gnawing at his soul. If Peregrino had been an ordinary dog like any other dog, all those feelings would not bother him in the slightest. What's more, he would not even have those feelings. But being an enlightened dog has its disadvantages.

"We will be back!" said Lucky, feeling lively and with a new sparkle in his eyes. "I promise you we will be back; I want to go duck hunting with you, I want to see the green pond, and I want to try those goose eggs."

"That is a promise you must fulfill!" said Ares.

"Amen!" said Peregrino and immediately added, "so, no more sadness, no more flat faces."

"Flat faces!" exclaimed Nikus. Do we look to you like mentally challenged bulldogs?" They all laughed aloud in their own way, and their previous worries and sadness all consigned to oblivion.

"We would like to see a little more of the barrio," said Peregrino, harboring hope deep in his heart to find Pepita.

"Let's wait no more," said Nikus, and looking at Lucky eye to eye, he said, "How would you like a large bone, full of tendons, ligaments, cartilage, and a couple of hundred ants adhered to it?"

Lucky answered with a lip-smacking sound, which he always made every time anyone talked about food.

The boys had a great time, saw lots of places, and met new friends. But as is always the case when one is having lots of fun, time flew and the two days they enjoyed together felt to them like two hours.

A half-hour past midnight of the second day of games, play, and fun, Ares and Nikus walked with the brothers to the old house where Lucky had lived since he was a puppy. He went in through the hole in the fence and sniffed the surroundings.

Not finding new scents in the back yard, he went to the house's rear door and placed his nose in the gap between the bottom of the door and the floor and sniffed, barked, and waited.

Lucky wanted to say goodbye to the kids he had grown up with, but sadly, no one was home. He barked a few more times, but no one came to greet him. He then gave one last and long nostalgic look at the back yard and ran to join his brother and friends. Even if his human family had been at home, they would not have been able to keep him, not only because Peregrino undomesticated him when he healed him, but because they were inseparable.

"We will be waiting for you no matter how long it takes you to come back," said Nikus. Without another word, the amigos, standing on their hind legs, hugged and kissed each other.

The brothers left Ares and Nikus standing in the middle of the naked avenue, watching them go into the night. Just before completely disappearing into the night, the two brothers turned around, and there in the distance, they saw the silhouettes of their friends. The four friends wagged their tails as if they were human arms waving goodbye. The two brothers turned around and disappeared among the houses of the neighborhood.

DEATH BY MANGE

———•◆•———

Peregrino and his brother took an alley Peregrino felt was the same one where he saw Pepita last time. That day that now seemed so distant to him. Trying to get his bearings, he stopped for a moment. He was sure that was the alley where he saw Pepita. But the wind that moved the trees' branches and the creepy shadows cast on the ground by the waning moon's faint light, turned the alley into the eye of a swirl of ghosts that spun around Peregrino. And that made him lose his bearings.

Peregrino continued walking at a slow pace, not knowing where he and his brother were going. He kept his eyes peeled and his sense of smell finely tuned because he had the uncanny feeling that something or someone was watching them.

When they came to a spot where the narrow street divided into two narrower alleys, they found themselves unsure of what to do next. Unable to decide which way to go, they turned around, and after a short walk, they found the earthen path that would take them to the highway.

The two brothers welcomed the grassless ground, which felt warm under their paws. To the right of the path, they found a lonely and dying dog. The poor dog had developed mange, quite common in that part of the world. He had lost all his hair, and dry skin had formed folds in some parts of his body which bled and stunk where he had scratched the terrible itching. Moving or walking caused unbearable pain, so he had laid there waiting for death to come. But death played hard to get and made him linger longer than necessary.

Having lost all his hair, the dog suffered the burning heat of daytime and the nipping cold of night. Peregrino and Lucky, their hearts full of sadness, approached the dog to see what they could do for him. Because for dogs, unclean, unhealthy, and loathing are not part of their vocabulary. Peregrino and Lucky licked the dog's body, trying to heal his wounds, but that was a futile effort. Under the unpleasant smell that emanated from the dog's damaged body, they picked up the almost imperceptible scent of their brother Niño. Seeing their brother tremble, they lay side by side, leaving Niño in the middle.

Peregrino managed to get his head underneath his dying brother, and Lucky placed his on top of Niño's back. Niño felt the comfortable warmth of his brothers and stopped trembling. Only then he understood why death had made him wait so long. With a thankful heart, he wanted to let his brothers know that he recognized them by wagging his tail, but it had ceased functioning. His heart smiled for the last time, and he was gone.

The dryness in his eyelids did not allow Niño to close the windows of his soul, so he left them open, like when one leaves his bedroom windows open on a warm night.

Peregrino and Lucky had fallen asleep and did not notice when their brother died. They slept for a few minutes close to Niño's dead body, and in that short lapse of time, they dreamed the same dream. They dreamt that they were running happily with Niño in an endless prairie of endless dandelions, in a world where pain, suffering, thirst, hunger, and cold were nonexistent. There was only the joy to run and play untiringly.

Dawn had not yet been born when they came out of their short dream. Even though they knew that Niño was there no more, they said their goodbyes.

"Goodbye, my boy," said Lucky.

"Fare thee well, Niño," said Peregrino.

Having the certainty that their brother was already in a better place; they went on their way to the highway. When they arrived at the six-lane road, Peregrino went directly to where he had left Mona's body. He sniffed the surrounding area, but all he found was a street dog recently killed.

With the smell of death in his nose, and his head full of sad memories, Peregrino and his brother nervously crossed the highway. There were not many cars at that time of the morning, so they got to the other side safe and sound. There, the handsome devil of the highway was waiting for them. "Good morning, brother Lucky," said Guapo mockingly.

And then he said in an ironic way, "How would you like a large bone, full of tendons, ligaments, cartilage, and a couple of hundred ants adhered to it?"

Lucky gaped at the beautiful dog, totally confused. He became even more confused when Guapo said, "Those were the last words of your dear friend Nikus … Demus. Just before he bit the dust under the tires of a truck. Said Guapo while giving Nikus a nickname. And then he continued saying in a sarcastic way. I thought you would be thrilled to know it."

Peregrino pounced on Guapo with unsheathed fangs, but Guapo made Peregrino move in slow motion so he would have lots of time to disappear. But, before he could vanish, he saw something in Lucky that caught his attention and wanted to take a better look, but it was too late, and he disappeared into thin air, but his unpleasant words and his ill-omened announcement lingered.

THE TENT OF AN IMPOVERISHED CIRCUS

———✦———

Peregrino turned around and was beginning to descend one of the almost vertical cliffs of the ravine when he heard a sad and imperceptible

"Pere" that brought memories of his puppyhood. Lucky was the only one that called him Pere in their early days. Peregrino turned around to see his brother, who was standing at the top of the cliff, looking at him with sad eyes. "Shouldn't we go back to see if Nikus is okay?"

"That's exactly what Guapo wants us to do," said Peregrino.

"Guapo?" asked Lucky.

"Yes, Guapo. That is how they call that evil being," said Peregrino.

"I assure you, brother, that not only our dear friend Nikus is well, but at this very moment, he is snoring loudly as well." Lucky smiled, satisfied with his brother's answer, and happily followed him down the garbage dump. There they stopped to eat a few chicken bones they found and shared the contents of a soiled disposable diaper.

The sun came out rosy cheeked, accompanied by myriads of golden butterflies, and was splashing the horizon with gold and silver when the two brothers arrived at Peregrino's den.

They sniffed his den thoroughly.

When they were sure there was nothing out of the ordinary, they turned around in circles as if they were trying to sniff their tail ends. That done, they let their bodies gently fall to the ground. Before Peregrino's body hit the ground, he was fast asleep and immediately he found himself in a strange world that was shrouded in a yellowish-green murk.

The change of scenery was so sudden, that Peregrino looked around, startled and confused, trying to find Lucky. But all he could see were his paws and his paws' prints in a light grey ground and as soft as baby powder. Trying to find his bearings, he looked up at the sky, which appeared to him like the discolored and full of holes old tent of an impoverished circus, where a few and diffused light shafts dimly lit that strange atmosphere.

Peregrino heard the whispering of running water. Following the faint sound, he came to a river whose waters were so crystalline and bright that they looked like liquid crystals.

The river's water was tempting and beautiful but devoid of life. There was not a single fish or a snail there, not even a solitary tadpole.

It was a deep river, yet Peregrino felt he could grab the gleaming pebbles from the bottom with his teeth by just stretching his neck.

He was so thirsty that his tongue was hanging out, imploring a sip of water, but there was something insidious in that river that made him nervous. The overpowering thirst made him overcome his fear, and he approached the river to drink, but at the last moment he recoiled in fear.

Suddenly, the wind swept into the water something that looked like dry leaves, and immediately it turned into an ice sculpture. With fear gripping his heart, he bolted away from the river.

It was high noon when Peregrino woke up the following day. He opened his eyes very slowly, and there in front of him was his brother, gazing at him. When Lucky saw that his brother was awake, he went to kiss him, got his head under his brother's chest, and helped him get up while wagging his tail joyfully.

It was a sweltering hot day. Peregrino took his brother to the small pond where they spent a long while lying in the water. When they heard the complaining of their stomachs, they appeased their hunger with the meat of some crabs and some small fish they caught.

Peregrino spent the rest of the day showing his brother the two realms of the ravine. Lucky was amazed; he could not believe that his brother was the possessor of all that beauty and wealth. "It is yours and mine; it is Pepita's legacy."

"Pepita!" exclaimed Lucky. "Whatever became of her?"

"She is somewhere around Ares and Nikus' ... Demus' neighborhood." Lucky gave his brother a quizzical look. And then they threw themselves on the ground laughing in their own way, as they remembered the nickname Guapo gave their friend.

THE COW

———◆———

A few months had passed since the day Peregrino had brought his brother to the two realms of his ravine. Since that day, they became inseparable, so when Peregrino awoke one morning, he thought it odd that his brother was not sleeping by his side as always.

He got up and went looking for Lucky. When the birds nested in the leaf litter saw him coming, they flew out, flapping their wings loudly and making a big commotion. This alerted the parakeet flocks and the parrot flocks as well.

The racket made by parakeets and parrots was so loud that every single bird nesting in the limbs of the trees or in the bushes flew out and joined one flock or the other.

The countless birds descended to the raging river at the bottom of the chasm, where they flew along the banks a short distance. Making an earnest effort, they flew back to the jungle. Once there, the parrots engaged in their usual fights, and after many karate-winged chops, screeches, and pecks, the wilderness was peaceful once more.

After thoroughly searching every nook and cranny, and not finding his brother, Peregrino decided to go to the garbage dump to find him. As he was walking around the small pond, he saw Lucky coming out of the secret passage, and behind him, with slow and hesitant steps, a young and chubby female dog came.

She was white with black spots covering her body, making her look like a miniature Holstein cow. Peregrino ran toward her, his lips peeled back so she could see his canines. He was not going to let anyone come to invade his secret paradise.

When the miniature cow saw Peregrino's ferocious face, she immediately threw herself to the ground. She got her tail between her hind legs and tried to bury her head under her front legs. Her body adopted a submissive position while she shrieked in terror.

Peregrino came hard and furious to stand over her, his fangs only centimeters from her neck, waiting for her to make a wrong move so he could kill her. The miniature cow knew it and did not move a single muscle, but her sharp shrill was louder than Peregrino's snarling.

All that fury, all that hostility in Peregrino, needed an escape, Lucky knew it. So, slowly and very carefully, he covered the miniature cow with his body while meekly trying to lick his brother's face.

Lucky's behavior pushed Peregrino beyond his limits of tolerance. Blind with rage, he seized his brother by the scruff of his neck and threw him on the ground. He shook him violently, giving him several cuts and bruises.

Lucky lay on the ground screaming in pain and whining like a puppy. Peregrino, feeling guilty, went to lick his brother's face, begging for his forgiveness.

Lucky, taking advantage of his brother's guilty feelings, jumped up and wagging his tail, kissed Peregrino on the mouth. Happy to see that the rage that had taken over his brother was gone, he playfully pushed Peregrino little by little to where the miniature cow was lying on the ground in a pool of her own urine.

Peregrino sniffed her urine and her genitalia. When he finished sniffing her from head to toe, he ordered her to get up. She got up slowly, shook her body vigorously, and shyly approached Peregrino. She thanked him for sparing her life and acknowledged him as her lord. Immediately after that, she proceeded to lick his face, mouth, and ears in such a sensual way that Peregrino was not able to move.

Nothing and nobody had prepared him for the feelings stirring inside of him. He did not want his brother and the mini cow to notice his shyness, but he did not know what to do; he just stood there, unable to move.

Lucky, enjoying every moment of his brother's incertitude, approached him and whispered, "Cover her urine with your own and then kiss her on the mouth, so she knows you welcome her into your family." Peregrino followed Lucky's instructions, and then he ran to catch up with his brother, who was walking at a brisk pace toward their lair.

Not wanting Cow to listen to what he wanted to ask Lucky, Peregrino whispered to his brother, "Where did you learn these rituals?"

"The master of the house where I grew up used to watch a box called television, where he used to watch a story called *Sex of the Animals*. He liked it very much; I found it fascinating."

Peregrino did not understand, not even half of an iota of what his brother said. But he was satisfied with his answer.

Cow admired her surroundings, and she liked what she saw.

Well, she thought, *Lucky was not lying about this place, and he protected me as he promised. Peregrino did not kill me; I think I love them both.* She then remembered a saying someone told her once: *A girl never knows what life has in store for her* as she turns around in some bushes. She then went following the two brothers with a coquettish gait, and then they were three.

FINAL JUDGMENT

O ne morning, three months after Cow joined them, Peregrino, Lucky, and Cow spent several hours searching for anything to eat in the garbage dump, but that morning, Lady Luck was not on their side.

Being so hungry, they decided to climb up to the top of the slope that was the garbage dump. There, Cow found a cardboard box with several soiled disposable diapers, the contents of which were hot, thanks to the morning sun's heat. And that was all they ate that morning.

Turning around, they were ready to go back to the jungle when a gust of wind hit their noses. Riding on the wind was Pepita's scent.

When Lucky recognized that scent, out of his mouth came a loud bark of unadulterated happiness. He immediately turned around to see Peregrino, but Peregrino was not there anymore. He was running at full speed toward the small cave while barking excitedly.

Lucky ran and barked like he had never before run and barked in his life. Cow did not know what was happening, but she did not wait to find out. She ran after the boys, barking very loudly as well.

Pepita came out of her den to see what all the commotion was all about in her neighborhood. When she saw Peregrino coming at her at full speed, it was too late for her to move out of the way. And she was hit and run over by Peregrino.

The two of them hit the ground violently and went rolling and tumbling. Pepita screamed in pain as she rolled over and over. Peregrino jumped up, his heart bursting at the seams with pure love and happiness, and licked, kissed, and hugged Pepita with joy.

Pepita was so happy to see her son that she completely forgot about her pain. She got up, only to be tackled once again by a meteorite named Lucky. Mother and son went tumbling down the steep slope. Luckily for them, they crashed into the trunk of a pine tree.

If it were not for that tree trunk, they would have tumbled to the bottom of the steep hillside, which would have been quite painful, or they might not feel pain at all; they would have walked cleanly and painlessly into the next world.

Pepita could not move because of the painful double impact and the weight of all the happiness in the world. Lucky pounced and pinned her to the ground, where he licked, kissed, and hugged her while whining like a little puppy.

When they had enough kissing and licking, they went inside the small cave with their tails on automatic and at full throttle. Once inside the cave, Pepita went to the far wall where Lucky and his siblings were born. At that spot, four little puppies were moving around and whining, looking for their mother.

As soon as Pepita lay down with her babies, they grabbed a teat with remarkable avidity as if those teats were lifesavers in a stormy sea. They drank their mother's milk greedily as if their life depended on it.

When Pepita finished feeding her babies, she let her elder children play with them. Peregrino and Lucky licked and kissed the little ones and allowed them to sink their sharp little teeth in their paws. It was then that Pepita picked up the scent of Cow on her sons. Trying to find the source of that scent, she got out of the small cave.

Cow had arrived at the cave the moment Pepita and Lucky went tumbling down the steep hill. She immediately picked up the scent of the babies. Knowing how dangerous it is to hang around a lair full of babies, she hid behind some bushes near the cave.

When Pepita came out of her den trying to find the source of the scent on her older children, she saw Cow standing a few feet from the cave's entrance. Pepita approached her slowly. When Cow saw Pepita coming in her direction, she nervously laid down on the ground and adopted a submissive position while timidly wagging her tail.

Pepita sniffed her, and when she picked up her sons' scent on her, she licked her mouth, welcoming her into her clan. That done, Pepita invited her to join her family inside her den. When they were inside, Pepita said to Cow, "Mi casa es tu casa. My home is your home."

As soon as all of them were in the cave, Lucky, who could not hold his tongue any longer, began telling his life story. When he finished, he said excitedly, "Now let me tell you about the fantastic adventure of Peregrino."

Lucky looked at his brother to see if he approved. Peregrino nodded happily.

Lucky told Peregrino's story, and in that story were Mona, Niño, Ares, Nikus, and the lady of the Halfway to Heaven Hotel.

When Lucky finished telling the two stories, all of them ended up with bittersweet feelings.

Pepita got up very slowly, not wanting to wake the babies up. When she moved away from her babies, she said to Lucky and Peregrino, "We must celebrate that you two are alive. This calls for Chinese food."

No sooner had she finished saying "Chinese food" than Lucky was already making that clicking sound with his mouth that he loved to do every time someone talked about food.

"Where are we going to find Chinese food around here?" asked Cow.

"I will show you the way, sweetie," said Pepita.

Fifteen minutes from the ravine at a fast pace, give or take a couple of minutes, there was a gas station and right next to it was a Chinese restaurant, where the prices and food quality were low.

The trash cans were at the rear of the restaurant and, fortunately for the dogs, one of the trash cans was full of food.

Food quality in the restaurant was so poor that the diners would not have noticed the difference if the waiters had served directly from the trash cans instead of from the kitchen.

The dogs greedily ate overcooked noodles, mushy steamed rice, and watery shrimp Chow Mein, with shrimp so tiny that they looked more like rolled-up millipedes.

Pepita bit into a fortune cookie and spat the little paper inside it, which read: "Beware of people announcing judgment day." Pepita looked at the little piece of paper, and even though she could not read, she would not swallow that saying.

Lucky found a paper bag full of egg foo young, smothered in curry and sweet and sour sauces, and that reminded him of the warm contents of the soiled disposable diapers.

The dogs, being street dogs, knew full well that such significant quantities of food were not an everyday occurrence for them, so they ate and ate and ate some more.

When their stomachs felt like they were going to burst open, they moved sluggishly away from the trash cans and let their bodies fell to the ground. Before their bodies touched the ground, they were in the arms of sleep.

They slept peacefully for a long while. Suddenly, Pepita had a dream in which she saw herself vomiting the fortune cookie she had eaten. Out of the cookie came the little paper. When she looked closely at the prophecy written there, it turned into a snake, and it bit her nose.

Pepita woke up startled and exclaimed, "My babies!" And she was already flying toward her den. Cow and the boys were running by her side. Pepita had woken with a sense of foreboding and was sure something terrible was happening to her babies.

Anguish squeezing her heart, Pepita took a shortcut that would take them to the ravine in less than half the time.

When they approached the ravine's edge, a disgusting smell penetrated their noses. At once, Pepita, Lucky, and Peregrino recognized that stench. The hair on their backs stood on end, and their teeth were at the ready. Who or what they had to kill, Cow did not know, but she bared her fangs.

When they reached the edge of the ravine, they came face to face with the inexhaustible source of the offensive smell. It was the monster that had taken Lucky and his siblings when they were just babies.

Their monster was a boozer who had reached the point of no return. He stunk of urine, poop, dirt, grime, and moonshine. He was a hairy man with abundant hair on his head, chest, and arms, and he had a long, bushy beard and mustache. He was smelly, dirty, and infested with lice and fleas and all kinds of vermin known and unknown to science.

When he saw the dogs coming at him in attack formation, the man panicked and at once threw to the ground the two babies he had in each hand. He then tried to reach the half of an old and rusty kitchen knife he always carried in one of the back pockets of his old, worn out, dirty pants. But he had run out of time. That day was his judgment day, and nothing and nobody was going to deprive him of that sacred right.

That day, those dogs became his judge, jury, and executioner. The dogs jumped on him; four mouths full of teeth closed in four different parts of his dirty, stinking body.

Boozer and the dogs went tumbling down the steep slope. The painful cartwheeling forced the dogs to release the boozer, and they went tumbling straight to the natural wall that divided Pepita's steep slope and the garbage dump.

The dogs hit the rocks embedded on the wall's face that were there like pimples and blackheads. They hit the rocks so hard and so violently, that they would have exploded if their creator had not given them anuses.

When they hit the wall's rocks, the flame of the fight, their soul, and their spirit went out of them, the Chinese food included. Senseless, not feeling anything at all, they went sliding downhill. Fortuitously, some bushes growing at the very edge of the semi-vertical wall stopped them.

The poor boozer was not as fortunate as the dogs. He went tumbling down to the bottom of the semi-vertical wall. When the dogs regained consciousness, they slowly and painfully got up and licked their wounds, which was their way to heal them. With her babies on her mind, Pepita licked her wounds the best she could and then went up the hill, limping very slowly and painfully.

Peregrino and company did not think their bodies could take the gruesome task of ascending Pepita's steep slope and then descending through the garbage dump. They had to go and make sure their monster was dead, so they decided to risk their hide by going down through the dangerous shortcut on the semi-vertical wall.

When they finally made it to the foot of that wall, they found the poor boozer between the sharp rocks that looked like the teeth of a gigantic fearsome beast. The dogs sniffed the man thoroughly, and soon declared him clinically dead.

Never again would he steal puppies. Never again would he make money telling the same lies the kidnappers of the barrio tell when selling the human babies they have kidnaped.

"These babies are orphans," they would say. "They are for adoption," they would say. "We do not do this for personal gain, we do it out of love. We want these innocent creatures to go to a home overflowing with love; the money we make is for their health care, food, clothing, and legal representation."

If those innocent creatures were to fall into the wrong hands, in the hands of wolves in sheep's clothing, the kidnappers would do like Pontius Pilate, wash their hands.

The dogs knew that their bodies, battered and bruised by the blows given to them by the rocks in the face of the wall, could not make the demanding task of climbing to Pepita's den. So they went through the portal that connected the two worlds of the ravine and spent the night in the tranquility of the jungle.

ZEUS THE BEAST AND THE KEY HOLDER

---◆---

T he day after the poor boozer's judgment day, it came in the hands of Zeus. Lightning, thunderclaps, and thunderbolts illuminated a stormy sky full of ominous dark clouds, announcing the arrival of the rainy season. The rainy season refused to wait half of a second more, and it rained heavily.

The dogs saw the rainstorm as the perfect excuse to remain in bed. Every bone in their bodies was sore, and so was every single muscle. They were so sore, that they felt sure that every single hair on their bodies hurt as well.

The torrential rain turned itself into a storm of hurricane-force winds that lasted all day and all night. At dawn the wind ceased; nonetheless, the rain continued.

Even though their lair was sun and rainproof, it was full of water. They were thoroughly soaked. They were so wet that the fleas in their coats were weaving a boat with dog's hair, so they could survive the deluge and perpetuate their species.

The rainstorm stopped early the morning of the second day as suddenly as it had begun. The immeasurable red-hot ball appeared in the sky. It came as fierce as a dog taking back its usurped territory. The sun was searing the land and turning the wetness into a fog that completely covered the huge ravine, turning it into a milky lake.

The fog rose gradually like earth's breath, allowing the sun to be the god of the land. Myriads of birds flew around the forest, greeting the sun god. They flew around the forest shouting aloud, "Get up, get up, you children of Mother Earth, our sun god has arrived. Love him, worship him, rejoice."

Peregrino and company got up from their waterbed very slowly, painfully, and shivering. Their first steps out of their den required a tremendous effort. Their limbs were too stiff because of the physical trauma caused by their violent tumbling down the steep hill. The injuries inflicted on them by the rocks on the face of the wall had numbed their muscles and bones.

At a slow pace, they went through the secret passage and headed to the garbage dump. At the garbage dump, Cow found an old mattress being steam cleaned by the burning sun rays. The moment they lay on that mattress, they felt that it was the softest, warmest, and most comforting thing in the entire world.

They rolled on the steaming mattress and rubbed their bodies on it, and in less than thirty minutes under the burning sun, they were steam cleaned, dry, and full of new life. They played and jumped on the mattress like human children for a short while, but when they heard their stomachs rumble, scolding them for the lack of food, they immediately climbed up the garbage dump.

Lady Luck smiled on them early that morning. They did not have to look for long nor climb too high. Out of nowhere, a cardboard box came rolling directly to their paws where it spilled its contents. They were astonished and could not believe their luck.

Peregrino and his brother were dumbfounded and could not speak. Cow exclaimed, "Mexican food!" They gulped it down with a voracious appetite—tacos, burritos, enchiladas, and a significant quantity of ground beef. The food was smelly and way too spicy for man and beast, but street dogs never complain about the state of the food they eat. Complaint does not exist in their vocabulary regarding food.

They ate till their stomachs were bursting at the seams. Peregrino and Lucky grabbed with their teeth one end of the cardboard box each, and headed for Pepita's den, followed closely by Cow.

When they arrived at Pepita's den, they found her lying down at the entrance of her small cave. Her gloomy-looking face told them that something was wrong. She wagged a listless tail at them as a greeting. When they approached to kiss her, they noticed her injuries.

Pepita had a nasty laceration that went from her forehead to the back of her head, and she had several wounds on her sides. The worst of her injuries was on the thigh of her right foreleg; there, she had a dangling ball of flesh, skin, and hair, which resembled a hairy keychain.

Peregrino placed the cardboard box at Pepita's paws, but she was in so much pain that she turned her face away from the food.

Cow reminded Pepita of the street dogs' first and second commandments, which helped them survive their lifelong struggles. They went something like this: "Thou shalt not turn your face away from food. Thou shalt not leave for tomorrow what you can eat today."

Pepita got up slowly and painfully, and while she reluctantly ate, Cow shooed away the swarms of flies that had taken possession of her wounds. Cow immediately began to treat Pepita's injuries, but not before asking the boys to go to the small pond to fetch water for Pepita.

The boys headed to the small pond, descending through Pepita's steep hill and down the shortcut on the semi-vertical wall.

When they were approaching the secret passage, Peregrino, the lead dog in that expedition, suddenly crouched down in the undergrowth to look ahead without being seen.

When Lucky, who was just a few steps behind his brother, came to his side, he saw three big and unfriendly dogs doing pee-mail all over the area, so they could lay claim to it and keep it as their property.

To his surprise, Peregrino saw his brother run and jumped on the biggest of the three invaders. He grabbed him by the throat and dropped him to the ground, where the dog's growls turned to squeals of pain and panic.

Peregrino and the other two invaders faced each other like medieval knights in a tournament. They sprang forward and gathered speed. Peregrino went speedily between the two invaders. One of the dogs, whose name was Belshazzar, sunk his teeth into Peregrino's back. The momentum of the attack made Belshazzar cartwheel and land hard on his rear end, but that did not cause him to loosen his grip on Peregrino.

The other attacker increased his initial attack speed and never stopped till he was out of the ravine. A piece of the dog's right cheek and part of his lower eyelid were hanging from Peregrino's fangs.

The invader who had landed on his rear end sprang up and, standing on his hind legs, tried to drop Peregrino to the ground. Peregrino jumped up, twisted his body, and fell to the ground, landing right on top of his attacker's face.

One of the invader's front legs landed inside Peregrino's open mouth, and he had no choice but to bite it, and bite he did till the bone cracked.

Belshazzar rolled his eyes up and opened his mouth simultaneously so that he could let out a scream as horrifying as the pain he was feeling, but not a single sound came out of his mouth. Lucky turned into a fury of teeth and hair, had him by the throat, and was shaking him like a rag doll.

Even though the dog was already dead, Lucky kept shaking him with blind rage. Nobody could dare to harm a single hair on Peregrino's body when he was around.

Peregrino made a tremendous effort to pry his brother off the dead dog. When Lucky finally let go of the dead dog's throat, Peregrino licked his brother's blood-stained face. For an instant, he felt the way he used to feel when he was just a little baby and Lucky protected him from the physical abuse his siblings handed him.

When Peregrino finished licking his brother's face, he looked at him and he thought his brother looked as if he was coming out of deep sleep. Lucky gave his brother a feeble and lethargic look and wagged his tail languidly as if he just came out of a long coma.

Lucky had never killed a dog before, and that day he had dispatched two to the shadows of the underworld, and that made him nauseous with an urge to vomit.

The fight drained all of Lucky's energy, so when Peregrino said, "Let`s go," Lucky had to make a tremendous effort to stand up. He then followed his brother in a downcast and slow-footed manner.

When the two brothers approached the spot where the lifeless body of the first invader that Lucky had killed lay, the dog jumped up and with blurred vision saw the two brothers coming toward him. The invader decided not to wait for them. Lucky unknowingly had left that dog half dead, when he had rushed to help his brother against his two attackers.

The resurrected dog, running aimlessly, still half anesthetized by his short visit to the underworld, reached the wall where the humongous dead three leaned upside down on it.

When the dog realized that there was no way out, he turned around. The revenant dog jumped over the narrow entrance to the secret passage and ran toward the garbage dump while shouting, "Assassins, assassins! You killed Belshazzar! Persians, Persians, I hate you Persians."

"Look at him run," said Peregrino. Lucky did not look. He felt relieved to see that dog alive and that made the air pass through his nostrils much more fluently, as if an invisible force lifted a ton of rocks off his chest.

Only after the dog had disappeared around the garbage dump and they could no longer hear the noise of empty cans and bottles rolling downhill, which the dog had kicked in his rush out of the ravine, did the two brothers go through the secret passage and into the small pond.

The two brothers rolled in the water to cool down and wash away the fight's injuries. As soon as they assuaged their thirst, they drank enough water to take to Pepita. That done, they headed for Pepita's den, where she anxiously waited. When they finally got there, they regurgitated the water one at a time at Pepita's mouth. She avidly swallowed as much water as possible, not wanting to share any with the thirsty, dry ground.

Cow did an excellent job on Pepita's injuries. She had also chewed and cut the thick thread of skin from which the ball of flesh, skin, and hair hung.

The following day Pepita felt much better, her injuries looked clean, and on their way to healing. Even though she still limped a little, she was walking, and hunger as her constant companion had returned.

Something is impressive and even miraculous in the saliva of dogs and in the way they use their tongue to heal injuries, whether their own or those of humans. It is a gift from Mother Nature to the canine species.

SMILING AT THE ABYSS

———◆———

wo weeks after the boozer had passed into oblivion, all the members of Pepita's clan were having a siesta, enjoying the coolness of the cave away from the sweltering heat and the scorching midday sun. Suddenly a frightening noise awoke them abruptly, with the screeching of tires and the crash of metal against metal and glass against glass.

The pungent smell of gasoline spilled on hot pavement flowed toward the ravine, along with an almost imperceptible scent of human blood which came straight to Pepita's and the rest of the clan's noses. They did not know it, but near Pepita's lair on the highway, a total of twenty vehicles lay smashed and scattered all over. The drivers of those cars had done everything humanly possible to be part of that accident.

Lucky's, Peregrino's, and Cow's curiosity was stronger than their desire to remain napping in the coolness of the cave, so they decided to investigate what was going on out there. As soon as they stuck their faces out of the cave, an explosion of heat surrounded them. Cow backed up into the coolness of the cave and went back to continue her siesta. Pepita, who was feeding her babies, thought it very strange, since Cow never missed the opportunity to be with the boys.

Lucky and Peregrino reached the top of a grassy hillock near the highway, where they had an excellent view of the road and everything happening there. From that hillock they saw uncountable ambulances and fire trucks, a lot of police cars, and hundreds of onlookers.

Cars going in the opposite direction had stopped. The drivers got out of their vehicles, but not to see whom they could help. No, they just wanted to see up close the crushed cars and the mangled victims of the accident, to give free rein to their fascination for the dead.

Suddenly, the wind changed direction. It began blowing from the ravine to the highway, carrying with it the smells of the garbage dump. The two brothers' scents sailed the invisible sea of the air. A couple of big dogs' curious noses picked up the brother's scent. The big dogs were in a cage made of wood and chicken wire in the back of a pickup truck.

Those dogs had been watching the two brothers since the very moment they had reached the top of the hillock. When those dogs picked up Lucky's and Peregrino's scents, they went mad and began barking and jumping up and down, trying to break free.

Lucky and Peregrino looked at each other with mutual curiosity in their eyes. They knew those deranged dogs were barking at them, but those dogs were nothing more than a pair of strangers. The two brothers' curiosity got the better of them, and they decided to approach the pickup.

The dogs' owner got out of the pickup. He was a burly, bad-tempered man, and that morning he was not in an excellent mood. The scorching sun and the sweltering heat, plus the fact that it would take the authorities a couple of hours to get the traffic moving again, had him simmering in a slow fire.

He banged with his opened hand the side of the pickup while shouting to his dogs to shut up. The dogs crouched down scared and stopped barking for just a second and immediately went back to barking and trying to get out of the cage.

To see the two brothers trying to climb up the back of the pickup was the straw that broke the camel's back.

The man, angry out of his mind, pulled the gun out of the holster he always carried under his left armpit and pointed it at Lucky s head. When he was just about to pull the trigger, he changed his mind. He remembered that his dogs were champion fighting dogs trained to kill.

What better way to kill time, he thought. It would be lots of fun to watch his champions beat the hell out of the pair of flea-infested street dogs and maybe even kill them. He slid the latch to open the door with a big smile, already enjoying the fight and the beating the street dogs would get.

Of the two dogs in the cage, one was male and the other female. The female dog had a white, shiny, curly coat. The male was black with large canine teeth and big, bulging eyes. Before the man finished sliding the door's latch, the door hit his hand hard as the dogs sprang out of the cage.

The black dog jumped on Lucky. Lucky landed on his back with the black dog on top. With all the power of his four legs, Lucky pushed the black dog, got up in a flash, and ran to the hillock.

Before Lucky disappeared behind the hillock, the man saw the black dog jumped on top of him, and immediately he heard Lucky's screams and desperate cries for help, which made the man laugh aloud.

The white dog jumped on Peregrino from the top of the pickup. Peregrino crouched down and moved aside. He then stood up in a flash and ran to the hillock to help his brother, the white dog behind him, snapping at his rear legs. The man was laughing his head off, completely sure his champions would swiftly kill the street dogs.

The four dogs disappeared behind the hillock, which was nearly thirty meters from the highway. The man did not follow his dogs; though they were precious to him, he trusted them blindly. He had invested a good deal of money training them and always fed them raw ground beef mixed with olive oil and chili powder twice a day. The dogs returned the favor by making money as guard dogs of a large shopping mall. The dogs also made money for the man Saturday afternoons as fighting dogs.

The man kept enjoying the fight even though he could not see the dogs. The man could only hear the growls of his dogs and the cries of pain of the street dogs, so he kept laughing, sure his dogs would kill the street dogs.

When the sounds of the fight ceased, he knew the street dogs had died or had managed to escape. The man stared at the hillock, knowing that at any moment, his dogs would come to him, but that moment never came.

Mariano, the dogs' owner, repeatedly called his dogs by their names, but they never responded. Fearing the worst, he pulled his gun out of the holster and went looking for them. Mariano refused to believe that a pair of flea-infested, poorly fed dogs could kill his champions. Still, that thought, like an earth tremor, reverberated with endless echoes in his cranial vault.

When he reached the spot where the fight had taken place and found no signs nor tracks of his dogs, he ran to the edge of the deep and humongous ravine. When the man approached the ravine's edge, he looked in the direction of Pepita's lair but saw those slopes were too steep; he did not believe his dogs were around there, so he ran in the opposite direction along the ravine's edge.

Mariano ran past the garbage dump and came to the spot where the giant rock blocked the way. He climbed the hand-chiseled stairs and reached the top. There he found some boys who used the lookout to hang out, smoke, and drink beer away from prying eyes, mainly as a place to be away from their parents.

When the boys saw Mariano's angry facial expression and the gun in his right hand, they scrambled to their feet and ran away, but not before answering negatively to Mariano's questions.

Devastated, Mariano approached the edge of the abyss. He looked at the bottom and fired his gun at it. When he emptied the magazine, he moved a few steps away from the abyss and sat down to cry like a little boy who just lost his favorite toy.

The moment Mariano sat down to cry was the precise moment the colossal rock was waiting to release itself from the ground's embrace. The great rock released itself in the same way one lets go of a lover at a parting, slowly and softly like one last caress, and it was gone.

When the big rock hit the bottom of the ravine, it twisted, and gathered speed, and went straight to the sheer vertical wall like a comet in a collision course with the planet Earth.

The tremendous impact brought down the humongous bulge that looked like a giant pregnant zebra, along with uncountable tons of sand and pumice, forever burying the dead tree that leaned upside down on the right wall along with the big rock.

Some of the boys who were brave enough or stupid enough not to be afraid of the stranger and his gun had gotten off the rock but hung around the ravine's edge to keep an eye on the man. They ended up enjoying the great show the giant rock offered.

When those boys went back to where the great rock used to be, they found a large black gap resembling the toothless open mouth of an old man smiling at the abyss.

When Peregrino and Lucky had tried to climb the back of the pickup to sniff those dogs that were barking completely mad in their cages, Peregrino and his brother picked up Ronaldinho's and Cinderella's scents, two of their siblings who had been dognapped by the man now known as the late drunkard.

Mariano, the pickup truck's owner, did not have the slightest idea that those street dogs he saw trying to climb up the back of the pickup were finding a way to free their siblings. The fight, the growling, and the painful wailings were a trick to fool him so they could escape.

Peregrino and Lucky guided their siblings to Pepita's lair, where they had a grand celebration. There were kisses and hugs, lickings, wailings, and howling of unadulterated happiness.

It was an immense pleasure to see Ronaldinho and Cinderella, thought to be dead, and now there they were, alive, tails wagging.

When all of them had had enough kisses, hugs, and lickings, Ronaldinho and Cinderella began telling their life story and their adventures from that day the boozer took them away to be sold, to the moment they had encountered Peregrino and Lucky.

When they finished telling every detail of the whole story, the hugging, kissing, and licking resumed. When the displays of love and affection slowly came to a stop, Lucky began telling his life story in that house where Peregrino found him.

He talked about the people who loved him and spoke of the children he grew up with from the day he was taken to that house by the puppy snatcher, now known as the late drunkard.

"For me," said Lucky, "that man will always be the hairy monster of my puppyhood. But no more will he hunt me down in my nightmares. One day, my family went out the door and never returned." He closed his eyes to visualize the children he grew up with and fell silent.

Peregrino took Lucky's silence as the signal to tell his story. He talked fondly about the Halfway to Heaven Hotel's enigmatic lady and wagged his tail excitedly when he talked about Ares and Nikus.

When he told the story of Mona and Niño, he lowered his head and his voice in sadness, and when he finished telling their story, he fell silent. Everyone in the cave joined Peregrino to honor the memories of Mona and Niño. All of them remained silent for a few minutes.

Pepita eventually broke the silence by saying: "It is now the opportunity for someone among us to tell her story. Someone we love very much, nevertheless, we do not know her story; we do not even know her name." They all looked at Cow simultaneously.

"Forgive me if I do not stand up, but I feel a little indisposed. My name is Belladonna; my friends call me Bella."

"Wow!" they all exclaimed.

"What a beautiful name," said Cinderella.

"Thank you, yours is also incredibly beautiful."

"Thank you, and please continue with your story."

"My life story is a sad one, and I do not wish to sadden this beautiful reunion more than the story of Mona and Niño has. I will instead share with you a little secret—Lucky, Peregrino, and I will soon have babies."

All of them looked at Bella with great surprise in their eyes. Except for Pepita, no one had noticed she was pregnant because Bella was a chubby girl.

Everyone in the cave was overwhelmed with happiness. Some of the family members howled, some wailed, and some of them barked. Pepita and Cinderella went to congratulate Bella and after a girls' only chat, Cinderella said in a loud voice so everyone could hear, "This we must celebrate."

"May I suggest Chinese food?" said Lucky, while making the clicking sound he loved to do every time the talk was about food.

"What a great idea," said Ronaldinho. "But where will we find Chinese food on these godforsaken cliffs?"

Peregrino and Lucky jumped on Ronaldinho and pinned him to the ground, where Peregrino bit him playfully while Lucky said to him, "We will show the way, blacky."

All of them, feeling genuinely happy, got out of the cave and took the shortcut that would take them to the Chinese restaurant in an instant. That time, Pepita's puppies joined that expedition; they were recently weaned and were famished. Thanks to the big accident on the highway, the restaurant was full of people and the garbage cans packed to the brim, so they ate their fill and then some.

They felt exhausted thanks to their overeating. When they were back at Pepita's lair, they huddled together for warmth and slept for a couple of hours. Suddenly, Cinderella jumped up startled, and loudly exclaimed, "Mariano!" They all jumped up, and only then Ronaldinho remembered his master.

The family reunion had been so remarkable that Cinderella and Ronaldinho had lost their perception of time. Still, there it was, back together with their sense of responsibility and fidelity.

The whole family, puppies included, went near the spot where they had left Mariano and the pickup, but they did not find one or the other.

"That is strange!" exclaimed Cinderella. "If he had left me waiting here, I would have remained here no matter how long he took."

They all nodded in agreement with Cinderella and simultaneously began sniffing the whole area. Ronaldinho picked up Mariano's faint scent right away but said nothing and went sniffing in a different direction.

When they were about to give up, Cinderella picked up the faint, almost imperceptible scent of Mariano. They followed it, and it guided them along the narrow path that ran along the edge of the ravine.

When they came to the large gap left by the massive rock, they found many young boys smoking cigarettes and drinking beer. Peregrino and Lucky were the lead dogs in that expedition, but when they saw the humans at the edge of the gap, they did not know what to do.

Cinderella and Ronaldinho were guard dogs and were afraid of nothing and nobody, they went straight to sniff the boys in the gap one by one in a very intimidating way as if they were cops and the boys a bunch of thugs.

One of the boys made the stupid mistake of trying to scare the dogs away by clapping his hands and stomping the ground with his feet while yelling, "Get the hell out of here, fleabags."

Ronaldinho and Cinderella jumped on the boy and pinned him down to the ground, while furiously growling close to his face and showing him their canines.

The poor boy turned completely pale and wet his pants. When the dogs moved away from the boy, he vomited his last lunch and early morning breakfast, and part of his last supper.

Pepita and the rest of her brood observed intently how Ronaldinho and Cinderella dealt with the boys in the gap. And that made their hearts burst at the seams with pride. Some of them barked, and some of them howled.

The puppies excitedly ran to meet Ronaldinho and Cinderella and gave them a hero's welcome. The grown-ups joined the puppies to give their heroes a hearty welcome as well. Despite all their efforts, they could not carry them on their shoulders as they would have liked.

The boys in the gap observed the dogs with great astonishment, then they went to aid the boy who had vomited and was still sitting on the ground with his head between his hands.

The dogs returned to the spot where the pickup truck had been, but when they did not find the pickup truck nor Mariano, they lay down by the side of the road to wait for Mariano, however long it would take him to return.

Well into the night, the sky presented them, free of charge, a spectacular show of lights followed by thunderbolts. Immediately after the show, the sky collapsed on them.

It rained cats and dogs and bulls and pigs as well. The dogs wanted to run home, but the torrential rain and the darkness of the night veiled their eyes. They could not even see the ground they were walking on, but despite that, they managed to get home, though not before sliding and falling quite a few times.

Once inside the cave, they got rid of the water in their bodies by shaking their haircoats vigorously. It was a small place, so the water they shook off from their coats landed on somebody else's coat. And the water somebody else shook landed on some of the others.

Trying to dry themselves the best they could, they rubbed their haircoats on the walls and the cave floor. That done, they huddled together to get some warmth and sleep.

Two of Pepita's puppies, Anaximenes and Anaximander, looked like identical twins. Even Pepita had trouble telling them apart. Those two puppies were inseparable, and their family saw them as one. Those two had turned Ronaldinho into their hero, and they became his shadow.

Ronaldinho had never felt so special, so important, so loved and admired. He had never been anybody's center of attention, and all that love and attention made him feel like a real hero.

That night of the storm, Anaximenes and Anaximander laid down close to Ronaldinho, one to his right and the other to his left side, leaving him in the middle. Ronaldinho hugged them and licked their faces, feeling happy and proud, and before they knew it, they were asleep.

Cindy, a coquettish, white-coated little girl dog, had picked Cinderella as her heroine. She imitated her every move and gesture. Cindy went to lay down by Cinderella's side, and Cinderella, feeling much delighted, hugged and kissed her, and after a bit of chatting, they fell asleep.

The fourth of the puppies was named Pirate by Pepita. Pirate was a brave and bold little puppy. He had a dark yellow coat with scattered and almost imperceptible dark red spots. One of his eyes was dark and the other bright grey.

Pirate had his heart and bi-colored eyes on Lucky. He loved and admired him, and nothing made him happier than to be near his hero.

Pirate threaded his way in the dark, stepping lightly on top of his sleeping family. When he approached the spot where Lucky was lying with his head on top of Peregrino's neck, the two brothers craned their necks in his direction. Peregrino grabbed Pirate and placed him between himself and his brother. Lucky hugged and kissed him, and they all went to sleep.

Morpheus, the Greek god of dreams, got inside the cave and carried the whole family in his arms into the realm of dreams. Once there, they dreamed that they were running tirelessly in a red soil plateau scattered with sharp stones and pale dwarf bushes.

In their dream, they saw the full moon hanging low in the eastern sky. Then they saw it gradually turning into the sun, and then the sun gradually turning back into the moon. As the days and nights came and went, the plateau turned into a desert.

Their dream brought them to the shore of a broad and deep river of a strong current. When they finished assuaging their thirst and cooling their feet in the cold water, they looked to the far, opposite riverbank. And there they saw a blurred silhouette that rose from the sand with the hot air bubbles that rose from the arid and blazing sand.

The silhouette disappeared in the air, only to rise again from the burning sands. Suddenly, they heard a voice calling each one of them by name. The voice sounded like a feeble and distant echo.

"Mariano!" Cinderella exclaimed. They all barked in unison, calling Mariano to their side of the river. The silhouette jumped in the water and tried to swim toward them, but it was dragged down the river by the strong current.

The dogs jumped in the river, trying to save Mariano, but the current dragged them underwater.

With their noses only a few centimeters below the surface of the water, and their eyes almost coming out of their sockets gazing straight at the unreachable blue sky, they moved their limbs frantically while trying to hold their breath.

When their lungs were about to burst, they snapped out of their dream, huffing and puffing. When they were fully awake, they felt the air pass through their throats, hot, humid, and saturated with their odors.

The whole clan went out of the cave to get some fresh air, but as soon as they stuck their faces out of the cave, the hot midday air impacted their noses like the blast of an old cannon. For a fleeting instant, they felt as if they were back in the desert of their most recent dream.

PARADISE LOST

~~~◆~~~

It was noon, and the heat was so oppressive that it felt like the sun was incinerating the earth. Lucky suggested they go to Peregrino's jungle. "It is nice and cool there and there is lots of water to drink and enough to take a dip."

"What a great idea," said Ronaldinho. "What are we waiting for?"

Cinderella glowered at her brother disapprovingly. "I am sure that is a beautiful idea, but shouldn't we be looking for Mariano?"

Ronaldinho, deeply disappointed, looked at Lucky, hoping he would say something that would change Cinderella's mind. Before Lucky could open his mouth, Peregrino said, "We all should be looking for Mariano."

Without making the slightest sound, they followed Peregrino to the highway. Once there, they laid at the side of the road, but the sweltering heat and their constant companions, hunger and thirst, forced them to quit, so they did not stay too long.

Pepita's clan had made Peregrino their leader, so they immediately followed him when he descended to the bottom of the ravine through the garbage dump.

Halfway to the bottom of the ravine, they found a cardboard box full of stale sliced bread. The bread was hard, but the clan ate it with gusto as if it were fresh out of the oven.

When they finished eating the last little bread crumb, Peregrino guided his family to the secret passage, but they could not find it when they reached the spot where the entrance should be.

The secret passage entrance was buried under the tons of sand that fell from the vertical wall when the huge rock hit it. Peregrino was devastated. He sat on the ground, not hearing or feeling anything. He refused to believe or accept that they had lost their beautiful paradise.

The puppies, who had heard so many stories of Peregrino's jungle and had looked forward to that day, were heartbroken; they threw themselves to the ground and cried plaintively.

The grown-ups kissed Peregrino and said they were sorry for him and for them for the loss of his paradise. But Peregrino did not hear nor see them; he just sat there not feeling anything. Suddenly, his nose picked up the tempting coolness of the jungle, and he heard it calling him, inviting him, casting spells on him with a myriad of tiny green voices.

The water coming down the face of the rocky bluff was talking to him with tiny crystal voices mingled with the music of the small pond's water nymphs.

Possessed by those voices and that music that only he could hear, Peregrino began to dig frantically like a hungry dog digging for a bone.

He dug like a pirate digs in a faraway island for an old wooden trunk full of gold. Like those old trunks full of gold buried in the jungles of Guatemala, gold Conquistadors stole from the indigenous people and then again from the king of Spain. They buried the trunks there, hoping to return one day from Spain. But that day never came; pirate cannons sank their ships, their Caravels.

Four legs, eight legs, forty legs digging, moving, removing, pushing, and pulling loads of sand. In less than four hours, they had uncovered the entrance to the secret passage. They were exhausted, but with an unwavering determination, they cheerfully continued digging.

The dogs lined up with Peregrino in the lead, and they began digging up the secret passage. The sand that Peregrino sent flying to the back landed in Lucky's face and on his chest, and the sand Lucky sent flying landed on Ronaldinho and so on, and so on. The sand went flying out from dog to dog to the last one at the end of the lineup.

When they finally opened the secret passage, Peregrino took his family to the deep pond, where they drank their fill and then took a dip in the cool water.

When they had enough of their well-deserved rest, Ronaldinho, Cinderella, and the youngsters that were anxious to see the rest of the jungle asked Peregrino to take them to the heart of it. Peregrino and Lucky were more than happy to give them a grand tour of their most precious treasure.

Cinderella and Ronaldinho were captivated by the sublime beauty of the forest. It inspired admiration and respect in them for its beauty and greatness. As they walked into the dense thicket, they became entranced by the exuberant greenery, making them stroll as if they were in a dream.

The day was coming to an end, and the rays of sunlight of that splendorous sunset that managed to filter through the tree's canopy came glowing faintly to the leaf litter, turning the forest into a magical place, into an incredible dream-like state.

The young ones, mesmerized by the vegetation that surrounded them, were helplessly attracted to it. The day became an ongoing adventure for them. The forest tour and the secret passage opening were fun for them. The junk on the dump scraped their legs to welcome them to the ravine, but they enjoyed descending into garbage dump.

Lucky made the clicking sound he loved to do every time he was hungry or when someone talked about food. Then he said that it was time to get something to eat.

The accomplished hunters of the clan—Pepita, Lucky, and Peregrino—decided to share their skills with the newcomers.

Bella disliked killing other animals or eating their flesh. She would rather go hungry or eat garbage instead, so she said that she was not the slightest bit interested in participating in that activity. That said, she turned around and headed for the den.

The puppies ran after Bella, and when they caught up with her, they said they would share with her anything they got. Bella thanked the puppies and hugged and kissed them; they reciprocated the hugs and kisses, then ran back to join the hunting party.

Pepita explained to the newcomers to the forest the proper way to hunt and fish. Lucky and Peregrino caught a crab each to show their skills to the newcomers.

The first of the newcomers to show what he had learned was Pirate. He caught a crab by flipping it into the air as if he were flipping pancakes in a frying pan. When the crab landed on its back, he grabbed the body and one of the pincers with his teeth; the free pincer found Pirate's lower lip and gave it a painful pinch.

The young pup jumped up and down as if he was trying to imitate a Thomson's gazelle while moving his head frantically from side to side.

The rest of the family enjoyed Pirate's show, their hearts almost bursting with joy. The grown-ups wagged their tails pleasantly, and the young pups rolled on the ground.

Pirate was just a young pup, but he stood upright facing his family with the dead crab hanging from his mouth. His whole body was an expression of triumph and pride that said: "Who is laughing now, eh?" Old and young alike jumped on him, pinning him to the ground, where they licked and kissed him, showing how much they loved him.

Pirate was just a young pup but knew how fortunate he was to have a family like his. He thanked each one of them, and because of the excitement, Pirate forgot Pepita's instructions and ate the crab he caught there and then.

Once the newcomers understood the lessons, the dogs separated into groups with a master hunter. Ronaldinho, Anaximenes, and Anaximander went with Pepita. Cindy, Cinderella, and Peregrino made up the second group. Lucky and Pirate went together.

When the hunt was over, they had caught so many crabs, birds, fish, and bird's eggs that they needed to make a few trips to their den to carry everything they caught.

The young pups, no longer able to hold their tongues, told what they caught and how. They talked so fast and so eagerly, and all of them at the same time, that it sounded like the words came out of their mouths and their ears as well.

The young pups were feeling happy and proud of their new abilities. Ronaldinho and Cinderella shared that feeling. That would be the first time they ate something that no one had handed them.

When everything was said and done and the feast began, Bella took advantage of the momentary silence and said, "I also caught something." All eyes turned to the trunk of the tree where Bella was lying with her back to the diners. Bella turned around slowly to show her family the seven tiny babies stuck to her teats.

The young pups were the first to welcome the babies by kissing them. Two of Bella's seven babies were black, two were white, and the other babies were shades of brown.

When Bella went to have a drink of water at the small pond, her babies blindly tried to find her. For an instant, it seemed as if Bella left scattered some of her colors on the ground.

As soon as the clan had their fill, and all of them had returned from the small pond where they washed down the food they had just eaten, Pepita said it was a good time to name the newborn babies. The whole clan agreed that that was a great idea and excitedly began thinking of names, in case Pepita chose them to give one of the babies an appellation.

Pepita began the name-giving ritual. The names given to the babies that day they would proudly carry the rest of their lives, even if they had to answer to any other name given to them by a human.

"Fortunato!" said Pepita while placing her right paw on the head of a black-haired baby of white socks and a spot on his chest in the shape of a horseshoe. Fortunato echoed the participants' voices. When they repeated the name Fortunato one more time, knowledge dawned on them that Fortunato was another way of saying Lucky.

Bella placed her right paw on the head of a white-haired baby girl that had a round spot around one of her eyes and said, "Alba!" As the chorus of dogs repeated Alba's name one more time, they knew it meant Dawn.

"Pure!" said Cinderella, naming a spotless little white-haired baby girl. "Pure! Pure!" repeated everyone.

Peregrino touched a light brown-furred baby that had some barely visible dark spots and said, "Niño."

"Niño!" came the loud chorus. Everyone went to kiss the baby named after their deceased brother. A short silence was observed in his memory.

When the silence was over, all eyes fell on Ronaldinho. He knew then that it was his turn to name a baby.

Ronaldinho placed his right paw on the head of a dark yellow-furred baby and said, "Alexander."

"Alexander! Alexander!" everyone shouted.

Nobody had to tell Lucky it was his turn to name a baby. He went to kiss a black curly-haired baby with very dark eyes and proudly said, "Eros."

"Eros! Eros!" repeated everyone.

After Eros was named, a silence fell in the den. When the silence was growing deafening because none of the grown-ups had any idea who should name the last of the babies, Anaximenes said, "Hayfield." Unsure if he was allowed to name a baby, he repeated shyly "Hayfield." With a great and pleasant surprise, all the adults looked to the spot where Anaximenes and Anaximander were shyly standing. But they never knew which of those two had spoken.

"Could we name that baby, please?" asked Anaximander.

"Yes, you can," said Bella, spellbound by the name which Anaximenes and Anaximander had come up with for the last of the babies. The whole family looked at the baby girl whose fur was the color of the dry hay of the country fields, and in unison repeated, "Hayfield! Hayfield! Hayfield!"

It had been a great and festive day for the whole family. A day full of surprises, new experiences, and discoveries. Lady Luck had accompanied them the entire day, and they celebrated with hearts overflowing with happiness.

The name-giving ritual finished, the grown-ups decided to stay in the forest. It was too late and too dark to carry the babies to the protection of the cave.

When the young pups heard the decision of the grown-ups to spend the night in the forest, they looked at each other and then stealthily moved away from the family gathering. Without being seen, they entered the thicket of the woods. They had loads of fun following tracks and scents and startling some of the nocturnal creatures.

Before midnight, thunderbolts and flashes of lightning announced the end of the fun. A majestic and ominous cumulonimbus silhouetted against the sky with the light of every flash of lightning, foreshadowing a rainstorm.The young pups, not wanting to get wet, sprinted to the lair; when they got there, they laid down to sleep next to their favorite brother or sister and they dreamed the dreams that young dogs dream.

THE SUN GOD

———◆———

The rainy season abused its sacred right to pour water on Mother Earth's face. The torrential downpour lasted for two days and two nights. Even though Peregrino's lair was sun and rainproof, the rain completely drenched them.

Thanks to her maternal instinct, Bella and her babies were dry. Bella had found a small hollow on the tree trunk big enough for her and her babies.

The morning of the third day was cold and foggy. Thick fog blanketed the whole ravine, making it disappear. The ground was completely saturated with rainwater and could not absorb a single drop more.

Unbeknownst to Pepita's clan, the ravine had turned into a mortal trap. Its steep slopes, its dangerous cliffs, and its bluffs were there waiting for gravity to give the green light so they could let loose thousands of tons of sand, mud, and rocks to the bottom of the ravine.

Once those tons of rock, earth, mud, and debris were on the move, they would drag down anything that stood in their path. The high, sheer wall gave the starting signal. It let loose countless tons of wet sand and rocks from its summit.

The wet sand and rocks landed on the bottom of the ravine with a tremendous explosion. The shock wave traveled around the grand gorge and beyond the highway. It was the signal for all hell to break loose. There were landslides, mudslides, and cave-ins all around the great ravine.

The dangerous streams of mud, sand, and rocks flowing down to the bottom dragged with them large trees and all kinds of vegetation, giving the ravine a new look and new and deep scars on the faces of the slopes and cliffs.

Sometime before noon, the sun appeared. It came as fierce as a dog reclaiming its usurped territory. It began vaporizing with its incinerating breath the fog, humidity, and the early dewdrops that came to rest gently on the petals of the few wildflowers that survived the mudslides and landslips.

The sun penetrated the secret forest as a silent and gentle explosion of warm light, as if a divine finger had just turned on the light switch of the sky.

Flocks of all kinds of birds went out flying in all directions, welcoming the sun god. They announced its arrival and shouted at the top of their lungs, "The lifegiving God has arrived! The king of kings has arrived! Long live the king!" They sang tirelessly all around the forest.

The clamor of the birds woke up Pepita's clan. They got up slowly, stretching their extremities to get rid of the numbness. And as soon as they recovered control of their bodies, they shook off the water in their furs.

The grown-ups carried the babies to a clearing in the woods so the babies could also welcome the life-giving sun god.

Thirty minutes under the sun were enough for them to get completely dry and full of life, willing and able to begin the morning hunt. That morning no one wanted to do anything that had to do with water, so fishing was out of the question.

When they were having a good rest after the hunt and breakfast, duty and fidelity seized Cinderella. She reminded Ronaldinho that it was their duty to find Mariano. Ronaldinho nodded in agreement, but deep in his heart, Ronaldinho was suffering.

Ronaldinho had secretly cherished the hope that Cinderella would forget about Mariano or that he would forget about them, but little did he know how much Cinderella loved Mariano.

Ronaldinho hated looking for Mariano, for if they found him, he knew that that meant the end of his new life.

Ronaldinho loved his new life because it made sense, and having a family vivified it, even if going hungry or eating garbage was part of it.

In Mariano's world, he had a dish and a jacket with his name on it, a comfortable bed, two good meals a day, plus little treats in between. But that was not a happy life for him. He was always indoors, obeying orders, following schedules, and working, which made him as unhappy as a blind person's guide dog.

Ronaldinho loved the ravine. There he was free to do anything he wanted. He felt it was his turf with his loved ones. There he was free to follow his dreams. Having a family gave him a sense of belonging. Being loved, needed, and admired made him feel truly alive.

Ronaldinho gave one last nostalgic look at the forest, then he breathed deep with his mouth wide open, imagining he was swallowing the forest and his loved ones to take them with him.

Ronaldinho went to kiss and say goodbye to Bella and her babies; he also kissed Pepita, who was there helping with the babies. When he finished saying his goodbyes, he went to join his siblings, a bit reluctant and gloomy.

Pirate was leading the lineup and was the first to enter the secret passage. When Anaximenes, followed by Anaximander, entered the narrow and dark alley, his nose hit Pirate's rear end, who was backing out of the passageway.

When Pirate finally got out of the secret passage, he turned around and faced his family who looked at him with inquiring eyes. "Blocked again!" he exclaimed; a bit disappointed because he had his heart set on the trip to the highway.

"Cheer up," said Lucky. "All we must do is unclog it again, which will not take us too long." And he disappeared into the dark tunnel. Lucky did not have to go too far to see the damage.

"It is terrible," he said when he came out of the secret passage. "And it is not sand this time."

The secret passage had been clogged by the mud, sticks, stones, bushes, and garbage as well. When he finished explaining every detail of the task ahead for them, he looked at Pepita. She had come to see what was happening.

Pepita took the floor and said, "Unless we want to stay here forever, which I do not recommend, we better start digging right now and fast. Because when that mixture dries up, it will be impossible to get out of here."

Peregrino planned the attack against the mud tide. "It looks like we will be here a long while," he said to the young pups. "I want you to go hunting, fishing, and get your paws into anything edible for all of us. When you finish eating, take a long rest because you will do the digging when our turn to eat and rest comes.

"Yes sir! Yes sir!" exclaimed the young ones. They then turned around and ran to the thicket of the jungle.

Ronaldinho, with a tinge of envy, saw the pups disappear in the greenery. He then turned around and went to join his siblings, who were already digging hard and diligently in a lineup, as they had previously done with the sand.

This time around, it was not as easy as with the sand; it was now a complex task that became harder as they advanced.

As they inched forward, large objects such as stones, bushes, and grocery bags full of garbage appeared under the mud.

They could not pass those objects under their bellies to the next digger; no, they had to pull them from under the debris and then dragged them out of the tunnel, which made them lose precious time.

The clan had to change positions every time they came across large objects. The ones at the front moved to the back, and the ones at the rear moved ahead.

The dogs moving to the back took advantage of the change of positions and went to the small pond for a drink of water.

Minutes before the day's sunrise, Peregrino ordered a halt to all activities. They all backed up, and one by one got out of the passageway. When the last one of them was out, Belladonna and the young pups greeted them with all kinds of fresh food.

"You eat and take a good long rest," said Bella. "You did much more than the lion's share; now we will finish the job."

"Where is Cindy?" asked Cinderella.

"In the lair babysitting," responded Bella as she entered the dark tunnel followed by Pirate, Anaximenes, and Anaximander.

When they finished eating, Pepita and her older children got into the small pond; as soon as they were in the warm water, a burning sensation ran from their feet to their heads. Only then did they become aware of the injuries and cuts from the bushes, rocks, and the broken glass hidden under the mud and garbage.

The dogs huddled together so they could rest their heads on the dogs closest to them and let the warm water not only heal their injuries but also soothe them to sleep.

The secret passage was roughly eight meters long, but Peregrino and company unknowingly had dug some eight meters more.

When Peregrino and crew had come face to face with several thick limbs and tree trunks dragged there by the titanic force of previous mudslides, and knowing that his crew was dog tired, because he was depleted of energy and unable to find a way out, he called a halt to all activities.

THE BRIGHTNESS OF VENUS

———◆———

The sun was twenty degrees shy of midday when Pepita and her older children woke up. Their bodies felt incredibly heavy, so they got out of the water very slowly. Peregrino and his crew had pulled out of the secret passage, in plain darkness, an incredible quantity of mud, garbage, and large objects. Now that they could see them in daylight, they found it hard to believe they had made that tremendous effort.

When Bella and her crew found themselves facing the bunch of limbs and tree trunks, she had the brilliant idea to dig up, using the limbs and tree trunks as a stairway. Without much effort, she opened a hole big enough for her to pass through it.

Bella felt incredibly happy when she found a way out. She could not believe her luck. She got her head through the opening to make sure she found a way out, and she looked at the sky at the exact moment when night's darkness fell to the ground, mortally wounded by the sun god's first arrows shot from the horizon.

Bella admired Venus' brightness for a fleeting moment. Venus was there, refusing to yield the heavens to the god of light and giver of life.

When Bella and the youngsters made it to the small pond to give Pepita and her older children the news, they found them deep at sleep, and they dared not wake them. Slowly and quietly, they went away.

When Peregrino and crew woke up that morning, they went to see how the job in the tunnel was going.

As they went through the hole Bella had opened, great happiness filled their hearts.

They stood around the opening spellbound, looking at the tremendous power of Mother Nature, as the landscape had been entirely transformed. Many pine trees and aromatic cypresses disappeared under uncountable tons of mud and rocks, as did most of the greenery.

The faces of the cliffs and those of the steep slopes had new and deep scars. The garbage dump was as though it never existed. There could not be seen even the slightest sign that there ever was a garbage dump.

Satisfied with Bella's and the kids' job, they headed to the lair to thank them. When they arrived there, they found Bella and her babies sleeping soundly. The young pups were nowhere around.

Bella woke up when she felt their eyes on her and got up, happy to see them. When they inquired about the young pups, Bella said they were doing what they liked to do best, hunting and fishing.

Pepita's and her children's muscles and bones were achy and sore, their feet were swollen, but their hearts were brimming with happiness. Grateful to have a great family, they fell asleep.

The young pups were heading to the lair with part of what they had caught hanging from their mouths when they met Bella. "I came to meet you here, not only to help you carry the food, but also to ask you to be quiet and not celebrate the morning hunt this time; our loved ones are asleep."

The young pups had become excellent hunters and were growing fast. They celebrated every hunt by dancing, barking, and howling as well. At the lair, they quietly put away the catch of the day, and under Bella's instructions, they took care of their brothers' injuries. Cindy took care of Cinderella's, and Bella took care of Pepita's wounds.

As soon as they finished their therapeutic labor, they all huddled together and slept. The darkness of the night quietly entered the forest. The nocturnal creatures stirred and slowly opened their eyes, and right away began the search for food, giving continuity to life in its night phase.

MARIANO

———◆———

Pepita's clan continued its survival tactics and its routine. They spent some days in the small jungle and some in the cave. Sometimes they ate Chinese food, other times they ate garbage, and still other times they went hungry. They always carried Bella's babies hanging from a grown-up's mouth wherever they went.

The garbage dump again had a significant quantity of residue, which was good for the clan because they always found something to eat. They always complemented their diet with the contents of the ever-present disposable diapers.

It was part of the routine to go to the highway to see if they could find Mariano. They would sit on their haunches atop the grassy hillock for a couple of hours, watching the vehicles flying by.

Much to the happiness of Ronaldinho, the day came when they decided not to go to the highway anymore. And they completely forgot about Mariano, including Cinderella, who was the one that loved him the most.

The torrential rains continued through the rainy season, and so did the mud slides, which kept dragging trees and vegetation to the bottom of the great ravine.

One foggy morning at the rainy season's end, Mariano parked his pickup truck near the spot where he had let Ronaldinho and Cinderella out of the cage. That day he was mistakenly sure his dogs would easily beat, or even kill those street dogs that were trying to climb up the rear of the pickup.

Mariano got out of his vehicle and headed to the back of the grassy hillock, where his beloved dogs had disappeared. He walked slowly with the help of a thick walking stick.

When he reached the back of the grassy hillock and saw the great ravine again, his heart leaped as he remembered his unfortunate and nasty accident.

In that instant, he saw in his mind's eye every little detail of the catastrophic seconds that his love affair lasted with the huge rock. In that same instant, he remembered vividly the moment the giant rock came off the ground's embrace. And he felt once more the horrible sensation of the free fall, which for him it was as if his testes had traveled through his guts and then lodged themselves in his throat.

Mariano remembered that before he lost consciousness that day, as he fell to the bottom on top of the rock. He spread his legs and arms and spread eagle went down on top of the giant rock.

The moment the ravine's bottom gave the rock the first kiss, it sent Mariano cartwheeling in the air and flying like the uncontrolled flight of a flea. Mariano was lucky enough to land face-first, and then went rolling and tumbling down to the bottom.

The boys who were smoking and drinking beer on the rock that day, and who out of bravery or stupidity were not scared to see Mariano upset and holding a gun, just got off the rock and stuck around, keeping a curious eye on Mariano.

When the boys saw the massive rock slip away from the embrace of the ground, they were scared silly, and unable to move. They watched the big rock's terrifying show with eyes and mouths wide open.

When the boys got over their frightening experience, they rushed to call the firefighters so they could rescue Mariano's body parts. They didn't think he was in one piece.

The moment the firefighters arrived at the edge of the dangerous abyss where the humongous rock used to be, they knew they did not have the right equipment for that job. While they waited for another truck to bring them the necessary gear to do the job, they stood around looking at the great ravine.

"Please take your time, boys," one of the rescuers said to his mates. "After all, some people die when they trip and fall on the sidewalk where they are walking."

"Some of them die when they sneeze," said another of the rescuers.

"Not to mention falling down a dangerous chasm like this one," said another of the firemen.

All that reasoning gave the rescuers the absolute certainty that whoever that John Doe scattered on the bottom of the ravine was, he was not simply dead; no, he was perfectly dead and three quarters plus.

Three hours later, they admitted Mariano to a hospital, where the X-rays showed eight fractured ribs and multiple fractures in both arms and legs. His nose was to one side of his face as if he were trying to sniff his left ear.

Mariano suffered lacerations and blunt trauma to his head and face and in the rest of his body. In addition to all his injuries, he had lost his upper front teeth. Incredible as it may sound, he was alive.

All of his injuries, plus the swelling and the death-like pallor of his face, made him look like a twin brother of the Frankenstein monster in Mary Shelley's book.

When he finished remembering and living once more his short-lived romance with the huge rock, he continued his slow pace toward the very edge of Pepita's steep slope.

Behind Mariano walked a giant of a woman, too tall and too chubby to be a native of that part of the world. She had a beautiful white alabaster skin that demanded admiration. Her reddish-blonde hair fell in cascades down to her calves, and she spoke broken Spanish with a British accent.

"Be careful!" his wife shouted when she saw Mariano approach the very edge of the ravine. "Remember what happened last time you were here." That said, she stopped walking and nervously watched Mariano from a safe distance.

Mariano stood on a ledge at the edge of the steep slope and stamped his feet to ensure he was not standing on loose ground or loose rocks.

Mariano spread his legs and stood firmly on the ground. He then filled up his lungs with cool air and whistled loudly toward the bottom of the ravine. He stood there listening to how the echo repeated his whistle.

When the echo died down and the ravine was quiet again, Mariano whistled one more time. The sound waves of the first whistle had entered as a whispering bird song into Pepita's cave, where all the family members were asleep and huddled together for warmth.

Ronaldinho was the only one awake. A nightmare where he had seen himself die a violent death had awakened him. The fear of losing his family had him there watching over them, gazing at them, feeling and loving them, suddenly realizing how beautiful they indeed were.

When Ronaldinho heard Mariano's whistle, his heart skipped a beat. He knew full well that the whistle meant the end of his new life. The new life he loved so much. Ronaldinho closed his eyes and pretended to be asleep, hoping Cinderella did not hear the whistle. Deep in his heart he knew that it was a futile hope.

Cinderella woke up startled, pricked her ears, and asked, "Did anyone hear that?" She said it half asleep and unsure if it was Mariano's whistle or one of her dreams where she often heard the same sound.

The whole clan got up and tuned into the sounds of the ravine. Before the sound wave in which the echo of the second whistle was traveling managed to get in the cave, the whole family was at the cave's narrow entrance.

Cinderella tried to run to the narrow cave exit but could not get out. Lucky and Peregrino had tried to get out at the same time through that narrow exit and were stuck, unable to get in or out.

The other dogs were crowding the exit of the cave very excitedly, trying to get out. So many stories had

Cinderella told them about Mariano that they wanted to touch and sniff him to see if he was real.

Cinderella's family knew that patience was not one of Cinderella's virtues. The moment they saw Cinderella coming with her canines peeled, they all moved out of the way, leaving Peregrino's and Lucky's rear ends at their own risk.

Cinderella sunk her canines into the nearest rear end, and its owner went flying out like the cork of a champagne bottle.

When all of the dogs were finally out of the cave, they saw Mariano a hundred meters away, standing at the edge of Pepita's steep slope. At that very instant, he whistled for the third time. The whole family barked in unison, calling him.

Mariano looked in the direction in which the dogs were barking at him, and when he saw Cinderella as the lead vocalist of that barking choir, he fell to his knees with his arms wide open and tears in his eyes.

Cinderella ran to him in a straight line across Pepita's steep slope. She was so happy and excited to see Mariano that she completely forgot about Pepita's well-worn path that would have taken her to the top of the slope in just a few leaps.

She made it to the bottom of the ledge where Mariano was kneeling but could not climb to the top. Mariano encouraged her with sweet words while stretching out his arms to grab her. Every time she tried to reach Mariano's stretched-out arms; she went sliding down. They tried and tried again and again, but their efforts were to no avail.

When she tried one last time and failed yet gain, Cinderella turned her head to the spot where her family was calling her. Only then she realized her mistake. But before she could do anything about it, the ground and Mariano went down to rendezvous with her.

A tremendous landslide carried them downhill. Mariano, on his knees, slid on the loose ground as if he were sliding on a giant slide, until he gradually disappeared.

Mariano's wife had stopped walking and was watching him from a safe distance. When she saw Mariano disappear in the dust, she fainted, and as tall as she was, she fell backward like a giant doll.

Seconds before the avalanche of loose ground, dust, and rocks swallowed Mariano, he managed to curl up in a fetal position, pull up his T-shirt to cover his face, and bending up his arms on top of his face and head, he tried to make an air bubble.

Part of the landslide stopped by trees and bushes growing at the edge of the semi-vertical wall; the rest of it slid down to the bottom of that wall and piled up on top of the sharp stones that looked like the lower jaw of a fearsome beast.

The positive part about the landslide was that it gave a proper burial to the clean bones of the poor drunkard. They were cleaned thanks to ants and other critter residents of the ravine.

When Mariano felt that the landslide had stop sliding, he tried to move his arms to see if he could swim to the surface for a gulp of fresh air, but the tremendous pressure on every square inch of his body would not allow it.

Not having any other alternative, he lay there motionless in that oppressive darkness, listening to how

Death digging and scratching like a mole, was rapidly approaching.

Death finds us all. There is no place to hide, he thought. That thought like a flash reminded him of the story of a man whose time to die had come. Death came dressed as a mailwoman to that man's workplace.

Knowing that that man's three children were waiting for him to take them to fly a kite and go for ice cream afterward, Death decided to let that man fulfill his promise.

Death appeared before the man and explained to him his situation. "I will allow you to fulfill your promise to your children, and tomorrow we shall meet at this same place and at this same time," said Death to the man. The man looked at his watch and saw that it was three o'clock.

The man thanked Death and promised to be at the same time and place the next day. Before disappearing, the Grim Reaper looked at the man with dark eyes, so dark that they reflected no light, then pointing a fleshless finger at the man's chest, said, "Do not dare disappoint me."

As soon as Death vanished, the man went to see his boss and informed him that his only living aunt was on the brink of extinction "so to speak" and that he needed three days off to go and make funeral arrangements.

The man got his three days off, but instead of going home to see his children, he went to hide at the small village where he was born.

When the man arrived at his village, he discovered that the annual carnival, which usually lasted three days, was about to start. The man could not be happier. Smiling, he thought, *Death will never find me here.*

That afternoon, the man went to one of the stores that sold carnival paraphernalia and bought a lady's pink wig, a pair of lady's high-heeled shoes, pink sunglasses, a pair of too-tight lady's blue jeans, and a very sexy pink tube top as well.

The next day the man, all dressed up in feminine garments and with his mouth full of chewing gum, strolled gaily among hundreds of visitors. He was sure that, if Death did not find him between the hours of three and three-thirty, she would have to let him live.

At three o'clock the following day, Death arrived at the man's workplace dressed up as a policewoman. She inquired about the man's whereabouts and learned that he had gone to his village to bury a family member.

At three minutes past three, Death arrived at the man's village dressed up as a female pirate. She began searching for the man. She searched high and low, but it did not matter how hard she tried or where she looked; her efforts were to no avail.

At three minutes before three-thirty, Death came to stand next to the man she was looking for but had no idea that he was the man she was trying to find.

At three-thirty, Death knew she had been cheated and had no other alternative but to let the man live. And that made her angry beyond her control.

Knowing that her superiors would not permit her to return empty-handed, she cast a sidelong glance at the guy standing next to her who was chewing gum in a very suggestive manner and was all dress up. Death thought, *I would take that thing with me; it is better than going back empty-handed.* Death put an arm around the man's waist, showed him her fleshless face, and said, "Kaput, baby!"

"Yes," Mariano thought, "Death finds us all." At that very moment, he felt an icy hand squeezing his heart very slowly; he knew then that the Grim Reaper had reached him.

For some strange reason, Death stretched his last seconds of life to an eternity. And that gave him time to reflect on what he had accomplished in his life and how short his life had been.

Mariano thought about how short a man's life is, even if one gets to live a hundred years. "After all," he thought, "what is a hundred years compared to the planet or the universe's age, nearly non-existing. Nonetheless, in that short time, one can do loads of good or loads of evil, but no one can do good or evil without doing good or evil to oneself."

That train of thought made him remember all the people he had killed in the Guatemalan Highlands during the internal armed conflict. Suddenly one by one, the putrid flesh faces of his victims circled his mind's eye— men, women, and children.

"I was serving my country!" he shouted to himself. No sooner had he finished saying "country" than the putrid, eyeless head of the old and feeble shaman hovered in front of his dirt-filled eyes.

The old shaman was the one whom he had decapitated with a single swing of his machete. The same old shaman who accused him in his most terrifying nightmares. Nightmares in which he always woke up sweating, cold, and shivering. The old shaman whose piercing eyes he had cut to pieces so they would stop staring at him accusingly.

The shaman talked to him through the mouths of the maggots that were devouring his putrid face. "That story only you can swallow; keep repeating it eternally so you can get to believe it yourself. But don't forget, the country is not only the land, the volcanos, lakes, or the jungle and its rivers; it is also the people. You cannot serve your country by killing your people."

No sooner had the maggots finished talking, than the piercing eyes of the shaman, the eyes that had seen the bowels of the underworld, materialized in their eye sockets. The eyes were those which Mariano could not shake from his mind because they were hot iron branded in the deepest part of his soul.

Mariano had encountered that old shaman seated on a rock outside the small village where he had arrived as commander of a platoon with the orders to burn the town and kill its people. "Mariano, I am waiting for you," said the old shaman in his native tongue.

As Mariano approached the old shaman, he mistakenly stared at the old shaman's eyes and was forced to look down. "How do you know my name, and how do you know I speak your tongue?"

"I also know what you came here for," answered the old shaman. At that moment, one of the soldiers approached Mariano to inform him that the village appeared abandoned.

"If you knew what I came here for, why didn't you run away with your people?"

"Run away where? To the north? And be mistreated, discriminated against, and forced to die in a foreign land? No! Better to die here in my land, in the arms of my forefathers."

The old shaman got up with difficulty and, staring at Mariano with eyes that had seen the innards of Xibalba, the Mayan underworld, said in a very solemn way, "I curse you, Mariano! From this day on and to the last seconds of your existence. I know you long for a large family like your father's family and like his father's family before him, but you shall always mate with barren women; your only children shall be dogs."

"It appears to me that you know much more that you should," said Mariano as he took the sharp machete off the hand of the soldier who had come to inform him of the deserted village.

"I know much more than you ever hope to learn, even if you could live two lives in a row," said the old shaman. Those were his last words.

When Mariano came out of his terrifying memories, he found himself shivering in fear and filled with repentance. He wanted to scream for forgiveness for all the atrocities done against his people, but he had run out of air.

One-thousandth of a second before he died, Mariano remembered that he had an unopened box of Haagen-Dazs creamy chocolate ice cream in the refrigerator. As he opened the refrigerator door, his jaw dropped when he saw Pope John Paul II standing inside the refrigerator.

The Pope was dressed in a Hawaiian shirt, shorts, and sandals. Seven little golden chains on his chest held a silver medallion on which an epigraph read in embossed golden letters: "The homeless could use a little bit of global warming."

John Paul was holding in one of his hands a tiny, golden bucket full of blessed water and in the other hand a damp cloth. "Your holiness," exclaimed Mariano, refusing to believe his eyes.

"Breathe!" ordered the Pope in a clear Guatemalan accent as he immediately began to wipe Mariano's face with the damp cloth.

Mariano opened his mouth wide and greedily gasped for air as he had done when he came out of his mother's belly. As he filled up his lungs with air and dust, a loud wheezing sound that sounded like the asthmatic whistling sound of the damaged carburetor of an old car came out of his throat.

Immediately after that, he was seized by violent coughing fits, expelling dust and dirt from his lungs, throat, mouth, and nose, and nearly popping his eyes out of their sockets in the process.

When he finally stopped coughing, he sat up. His face was a mess of dirt and dust. Rivers of tears had made trails down his cheeks, and there was plenty of saliva hanging from his mouth and long, sticky, slimy stuff hanging from his nose.

Mariano made a great effort to open his eyes. And with his vision blurred by the dust, his tears, and the sunlight, he saw Peregrino licking his face. When he finally was able to talk, with a very hoarse voice, he said to Peregrino, "Thank you, thank you, Your Holiness."

Stunned and quivering, he looked around, trying to find the Pope, but all he could see were four beautiful dogs diligently removing the last bits of dirt from his feet. Only then he remembered that Pope John Paul II had been dead for a long time.

Twenty meters down the steep slope, Mariano saw Cinderella coming up to him. She looked stunned and she limped. Bella and Pepita were by her side, encouraging her to keep walking. Bringing up the rear was Lucky. Ronaldinho was pushing his sister and making sure she did not roll down the slope.

Cinderella made a super canine effort and managed to reach Mariano's opened arms, and there she collapsed, her nose and mouth bleeding profusely.

Making a superhuman effort, Mariano forgot his injuries and pain and managed to get up with Cinderella in his arms. He began to ascend to the slope's summit, guided by the dogs.

As they walked by Pepita's cave, Bella's puppies, who watched the action and did not miss any detail, were sure that Cinderella's tragedy was Mariano's fault, so they barked at him with a menacing tone of voice.

Bella ran to silence them, and after assuring them that Mariano was family and that he would take care of Cinderella, they wagged their tails happily.

Despite the grief that filled his heart, Mariano could not help but smile. "What is wrong, my children?" said Mariano. No sooner had he finished saying those words than the image of the severed head of the old shaman appeared in his mind.

Mariano, having sincerely repented for all the evil, all the suffering, and all the killings against his people, shouted, "Forgive me! Forgive me! I am sorry! I am sincerely sorry! Sorry! Sorry! Sorry!" The echo resounded all over the immense ravine.

When Bella realized that her babies had joined their older brothers in the journey to the highway, she went to stop them. Anaximenes and Anaximander begged her to let them be part of that great event, vowing to protect them with their lives.

"Remember, Bella," said Anaximenes, "the sooner they begin to know the world they live in, the better their chances of survival." Cindy and Pirate joined their brothers, and they too vowed to protect the babies; seeing them so determined, Bella gave in to their request.

Mariano reached the summit, and as he took the first steps away from the ravine, he was overwhelmed by a feeling of freedom from sinfulness and guilt. *After all*, he thought, *I was a soldier following orders.*

As Mariano headed toward the highway, he saw his wife sitting on the ground surrounded by four women who were fanning her with their hats and giving her a glass of water.

When his wife saw Mariano leading a pack of dogs toward her and carrying Cinderella in his arms, she fainted again.

Mariano arrived at the pickup. He placed Cinderella lovingly in the back seat. Mariano was surprised to see Cindy and Ronaldinho getting in the back seat with Cinderella. He made sure the dogs were comfy, and after locking the door, he turned around to go and help his wife but was pleasantly surprised to see her approaching the pickup in the company of the four women who had assisted her when she had fainted.

Mariano hastily helped his wife into the pickup, thanked the women profusely, hugged and kissed the dogs, then briskly got in the pickup and drove off, disappearing rapidly among the other vehicles on the road.

MAXIMÓN (MA-SHE-MÓN)

———◆———

Pepita and the rest of the clan had stayed at the highway's edge, staring at the fast-moving vehicles as if in a trance, totally absorbed in their thoughts.

"Will the beautiful and brave Cinderella die? Will we ever see Cindy and Ronaldinho again?" Those were some of the many questions they were asking themselves and, without realizing it, they were unable to move, unable to feel anything; their senses had left with the pickup.

The four women who had helped Mariano's wife were engrossed in staring at the dogs, and without realizing it, they got caught up in the dogs' collective trance.

The women and the dogs had been in that weird trance where they could not move, for only a short time, when the traffic slowed down and stopped for something that had happened ahead on the highway.

A big truck loaded with sheet metal rolls stopped in front of the group of women and dogs who were there, seemingly not moving or not even breathing as if they were carved figures.

The driver of the big truck was in a terrible mood and sweating. When he saw the women and dogs standing there like life-size statues as if time had stopped for them, he got scared because he was a believer of evil spirits, witchcraft, apparitions, and a worshiper of the Mayan idol granter of good and evil requests called Maximón. Shivers went down his spine, and his whole body shook violently.

The man shook in fear like an ordinary street dog, and to drive away his fears and any bad omens that could come his way, he pulled the chain hanging in the truck's cabin close to his head, which activated the truck's horn.

That truck's horn consisted of six trumpets that were on top of the truck's cabin; when the man pulled the chain, the blast of those trumpets produced the same number of decibels produced by the explosion of the Krakatoa in 1883, making the group of women and dogs nearly jump out of their skin. To make sure they didn't go back to that hallucinating state, the truck driver blasted the horn two more times for good measure.

When the dogs got over the big shock from the powerful horn, they headed home, followed closely by the four women who had taken an interest in Bella's puppies.

"I know these dogs," said one of the women whose name was Julia. "The ravine is their home; I watch them all the time. They come to sit at the hillock by the side of the highway to watch the cars go by and to look at every car that stops at the highway's edge. I always thought they were waiting for someone. They stay for only a couple of hours and then return to the ravine; now I know they were waiting for the pickup man."

"I would love to take one or two of those adorable babies with me," said the second woman.

"It would be wonderful if I could take one of them," said the third woman.

"I want that cutie with the white socks," said Julia.

"I don't think that is a good idea," said the fourth woman. "Those are street dogs; they are practically wild and are not used to living with people. They could be dangerous," she warned.

"Nonsense!" said Julia. "Didn't you see how the pickup man hugged and kissed them? And didn't you see how they reciprocated by hugging him and licking his face?"

The fourth woman kept quiet, taking that as a win; Julia walked fearlessly among the dogs. She approached Pirate who was walking close to Fortunato. She caressed his head and ran her soft hand from his head to the tip of his tail.

Pirate liked that and could not stop himself from wagging his tail in approval. Julia mistakenly took that as a good sign and bent down and hugged Fortunato, feeling utterly sure of herself. When she was about to lift him off the ground, Lucky who was walking behind Fortunato, unceremoniously sunk his fangs into Julia's left butt cheek.

When Julia registered the piercing pain, her brain made her do three things simultaneously. First, she let go of Fortunato. Second, she jumped up, and third, she let out a loud, hideous scream of pain.

Julia tried desperately to get away from the dogs, but Pirate had one of her hands and was pulling her down. Julia involuntarily placed her buttocks on Lucky's face. *If they pierce one of your cheeks, offer the other one,*

Lucky thought, and sank his teeth into Julia's right butt cheek.

Julia did not know how she escaped from the dogs, but before she could get away, Pirate grabbed one of her shoes by the heel; Julia shook her leg frantically, leaving the shoe in Pirate's teeth, and ran away screaming in pain and fear.

Pirate approached Fortunato, gave him Julia's shoe, and said, "Here is a souvenir you can take home." Fortunato grabbed the shoe with his teeth and shook it playfully, his little heart overflowing with love for Pirate.

Peregrino, Bella, Pepita, Anaximenes, and Anaximander took care of the other women and that helped them get rid of the frustration they felt because of their inability to help beautiful Cinderella.

The dogs stood there with a big smile in their hearts, watching the women flee with their clothes torn and their flesh pierced.

When the women realized that the dogs were no longer interested in their flesh, they stopped running and began to lick their injuries, in a manner of speaking.

Julia, who was twice bitten and doubly sore, with rivers of tears streaming down her cheeks and drenching her blouse, said to her friends, "There will be hell to pay! Those stinking dogs will pay dearly for what they did to us." "You girls want to get your own revenge? Or shall we do it together?"

"I don't think that is a good idea," said Ana, the woman who originally warned them not to mess with the dogs. "Besides," she said, "It is our fault for messing with street dogs."

"Who cares whose fault it was?" said Julia angrily. "A nephew of mine belongs to a street gang; if we pay them, they will gladly come with knives, machetes, baseball bats, and whatever they can get their hands on and give the flea-infested dogs a beating. Maybe even kill a couple of them. After all, we live in a city of rampant violence, it is always good to befriend street gang members who are quick to apply their justice, which is much better than trusting corrupted and inept police officers."

Julia's friends concurred that the dogs' fangs had turned her into a prophet, because her words were full of wisdom and love. But they also said they wouldn't participate in that stupidity.

"Have it your way," Julia said to her friends. "But mark my words, when those stinking dogs come up to the highway next time, we will be waiting for them. That said, Julia went her separate way at a brisk pace, caressing her perforated rump.

The clan members were hungry and thirsty, thanks to the events of that hectic day. They headed to the garbage dump at the puppies' pace. The first thing they found was a large plastic container full of rainwater. They all assuaged their thirst; nevertheless, food was in short supply. After two hours of unsuccessful searching, Peregrino called a halt to the food-finding effort.

"Tomorrow could be a better day," said Peregrino. "Let us go to sleep." That said, he grabbed Hayfield by the scruff of her neck and headed to the cave, followed closely by Bella, Pepita, and Lucky. Each carried a puppy, leaving Pirate, Anaximenes, and Anaximander in charge of taking home Eros, Alexander, and Fortunato.

The youngsters had never taken part in that activity, and no matter how hard they tried, they could not do it. The youngsters, not wanting to fail to accomplish their task, pulled the puppies uphill

Lucky and Peregrino wanted to play a trick on the youngsters and asked the puppies to make the youngsters' task difficult, so while the youngsters suffered, the rest of the clan watched the action behind a bush, having a little bit of fun.

Dead tired and over-stressed, the youngsters made it to the bush with the puppies in tow. Pirate grabbed Eros by the tail and put him in the arms of his mother, so to speak.

Pirate, Anaximenes, and Anaximander threw themselves to the ground, exhausted but satisfied to have accomplished their mission.

The adults went to kiss the youngsters and congratulated them on a job well done. And then Pepita told them that Peregrino and Lucky had planned it as a joke; the youngsters jumped on their older brothers and bit them playfully. The whole family, forgetting their hunger and troubles, played a bit longer.

Two weeks had passed since the day Bella had weaned her babies, and that night she had no food to offer them. She was worried and sad to see her puppies whimpering and licking the adults' mouths in the hope they would regurgitate some food.

Peregrino, unable to bear the suffering of the puppies, thought aloud, "What about Chinese food?" No sooner had he said Chinese than Lucky, the youngsters, and the puppies were out of the cave, making Lucky's clicking sound.

When the dogs reached the back of the Chinese restaurant, it was late at night, and no lights or people could be seen or heard around the restaurant. They were lucky enough to find one of the garbage cans full of leftovers. Being street dogs, they ate and ate until they were bursting at the seams. They knew that food was not always readily available, and the following days may not bring any food at all.

The dogs' way of living continued like the current of a river, uninterrupted. Pepita's clan was not the spoiled dogs of some human, nor was their daily bread like manna falling from heaven. Their meals were not a sure thing; many days, they went hungry. Despite that, they were happy. Besides, going hungry for a day or two is good for man and beast. Going hungry kept them on their toes and looking svelte, even if they didn't know it.

THE BATTLEFIELD

O ne afternoon while waiting at the edge of the highway for the pickup man to return with Cinderella, Cindy, and Ronaldinho, Peregrino suddenly heard a thud to his right side. Instantly, he saw Lucky and Pirate jump up; as he quickly got up, something went whistling between his pricked-up ears, and only then he realized they were under attack.

A street gang of about twenty thugs came at them with slingshots, knives, machetes, sticks, and baseball bats. The gang members surrounded the dogs in a semicircle with the evil intention to force them onto the highway, where they would die under the tires of the speeding vehicles.

When the gang members saw the dogs coming at them with unsheathed fangs, they screamed like savages and stomped their feet while hitting the ground with their baseball bats, machetes, and sticks, making one hell of a loud racket.

All that racket did not frighten the dogs away; they were not cowards, nor skittish animals that would run at the first sound of danger. All of them, Bella's puppies included, launched into the attack.

Peregrino, Lucky, Bella, and Pepita spearheaded the attack. They were the first to receive the rain of stones, aluminum bats, and sharp-edged machetes. And that turned them from angry dogs into dangerous dogs.

Pirate pounced on one of the gang members and bit his genitals. The thug screamed in pain and panic as he fell backward to the ground. Pirate pounced on him once more, and that time he bit the gang member's nose. The hooligan's brain could not manage the pain and disconnected itself.

Pirate, supercharged with energy and fury, pounced on the next gang member, but three thugs brought him down with aluminum clubs before he could reach him. Pirate went rolling on the ground screaming in pain as the jagged edge of his broken ribs punctured his internal organs. All of Pirate's energy escaped him, like the energy of a lightning bolt escapes as it strikes the ground.

Pirate, unable to move, lay on the ground; when he saw the three gang members approach with their aluminum clubs ready to finish him off, he closed his eyes, resigned to die.

Suddenly, Pirate heard the roar of angry lions. Pirate perked up his ears. And when he opened his eyes, he saw Cindy, Cinderella, and Ronaldinho attack the three thugs with irrepressible fury. Flesh, blood, hair, and pieces of clothing were flying all over as if they were the feathers of chickens being ripped to pieces by hungry wolves. Pirate, with a big smile in his heart, closed his eyes and was gone.

Dogs and thugs continued doing battle. One of the gang members slashed Peregrino with a sharp-edged machete, leaving him with a deep wound that ran from his tail to his neck. Another gang member struck him with a big stick south of his waist, which made him sit. A third thug with an aluminum bat hit him in the head.

Peregrino fell to the ground, his four legs shaking uncontrollably. Without control of his body, he lay there helplessly, looking at ground level as far as he could see away from the battlefield. He wanted to keep his eyes open to the bitter end, but his eyelids, heavy as lead, were slowly closing.

Before his eyes closed completely, he saw a couple of red ribbons, which appeared like a vision or a strange dream. Those ribbons were dancing and jumping with the wind as if they were Chinese dancers, dancing in the hair of the woman named Julia, who was hiding behind a streetlight pole, enjoying the action from a safe distance. A gang member holding an aluminum bat positioned himself over Peregrino, ready to finish him. The machete-wielding thug that slashed Peregrino, a tattooed, shirtless, head-shaven man, shoved the guy with the aluminum bat out of the way and said, "Let me cut this one's head off."

The shirtless thug raised the blood-stained machete. When he was about to strike, he took a couple of faltering steps and fell to the ground with two bullet perforations on his bare chest, right where he had tattooed in large capital letters "M. S.," which was the name of his gang. The other two guys fell to their knees with two bullet holes in their abdomens.

When the rest of the gang members heard the seven shots fired by Mariano, they ran away, chased by some of the dogs that could still run.

Very slowly, because he still had trouble walking without a walking stick, Mariano walked to the spot where the three thugs he had shot lay on the ground.

When he saw the dog that had saved him from the landslide, the same dog he mistook for John Paul II, laying on the ground bleeding, and a few steps away from him five dead puppies, he cried out, "My children!"

With his heart full of hate and his eyes full of tears, he shot in the head the two gang members who were holding their stomachs with both hands. He then approached the shirtless thug lying on the ground in a pool of his own blood and staring at his feet. The thug's trembling arms were outstretched to the sky as he repeated, "The Bible, the Bible." The dying thug saw the Grim Reaper standing at his feet and did not want to die without the Bible in his hands, hoping that the Good Book would keep him from going to Dante Alighieri's favorite place.

Mariano aimed his gun at the thug's head, but when he was about to pull the trigger, he changed his mind and decided not to give the man the relief a couple of lead pills would give him, so he stood there watching disdainfully how the man's life ebbed away little by little.

One man out of the many who came to see the incident, found lying around an old telephone directory and placed it in the dying man's hands. The thug thought it was the Bible and squeezed it tightly in his arms and died, ceasing thus and only thus to be vermin to society.

VITALINO TAHUITE

M ariano was still watching the dead, shirtless guy when three shots rang near his back. *Too close to miss me*, he thought and instinctively ran his left hand along his chest. "Drop the gun to one side and hit the ground!" shouted the policeman with a clear accent of the Guatemalan Highlands, letting Mariano know where the owner of that voice was from.

Mariano had spent so many years in the Highlands training indigenous recruits that he had learned to speak two of their languages. He tossed his gun to one side and dropped to his knees, but with incredible agility, twisted his body like a cat and landed on his back, trying to see who that policeman was.

As Mariano lay on the ground watching the policeman approach while training his gun at him, he tried hard to remember that face. "Vitalino Tahuite!" he exclaimed the second he recognized the policeman. He had trained him at the army barracks when he was a drill instructor and Vitalino a recruit of only seventeen years of age and fresh from the Guatemalan Highlands.

Mariano made a mockery of Vitalino's language and his Highlands accent. And, slowly, he repeated Vitalino's first words in Spanish when he began learning the official Guatemalan language. Vitalino's first words in Spanish went something like this: "Where your house you live? How is your name you call yourself?"

Mariano's cruel mockery became a time machine for Vitalino, forcing him to travel in time in a matter of a thousandth of a second. Hand in hand with his childhood memories, Vitalino arrived at the small village where he had been born and raised until his seventh birthday.

As if he was watching a black and white movie, the images were passing in front of his mind's eye at the speed of light; nonetheless, he saw and remembered vividly every little detail of that heinous day of his seventh birthday.

In that thousandth of a second, he saw the small village lying half-asleep on top of a hill. That hill was relatively high but being at the foot of the great chain of mountains of the Sierra Madre made it look much smaller.

Three sides of that hill fell away toward the broad and gentle river that was wedged between the hills' sides and the foot of the mountain range. From the village at the other side of the hill, one could see the sowing fields and if one paid attention, one could see the farmers who were working there. At a distance, they looked like rag dolls.

That tragic day of Vitaliano's seventh birthday, the farmers looked at the sky, and as they saw the sun's position, they knew it was two o'clock, give or take a minute or two.

The farmers stopped their tasks and headed to the river where they had previously agreed to meet. The men got in the water with their clothes on, knowing that their clothes would be completely dry by the time they reached the village.

The farmers got out of the water and began the long walk to the village. No sooner had they walked twenty paces than a vision of a rider dressed in a black cloak and riding a black horse galloped past them at breakneck speed, pursued by a dust cloud. Thinking it was the priest, the men quickened their pace, totally forgetting that Death rides on a black horse in those God-forsaken places.

Vitalino was happy and excited that day, imagining that the whole village was getting ready to celebrate his birthday and not Saint Patrick's Day, the village's Irish saint.

Early that morning, the boys and girls had helped the women decorate the church with so many white flowers and bright green leaves that the church and the small park that was part of the church grounds ended up looking like a bride on her wedding day.

The village boys and girls gave the church and the houses, including the tree's trunks, a whitewashed coat. The narrow, earthen streets were sprinkled with water and swept with large brooms made of dry roots.

Once the men finished sweeping the streets, the women carpeted them with aromatic pine needles. On top of that, they scattered fragrant white wildflowers, making the small village look like a well-garnished vanilla cake.

It was Saint Patrick's Day and only Christmas Day was much more awaited and solemn than Saint Patrick's. Those were the only two celebrations where everyone in the village played a part in one activity or another.

The kite flying competition was about to begin; there would be prizes for the best designs, from the most colorful to those that flew the highest.

Chente was what Vitalino used to call his father because he never learned to call him Dad. A week before Saint Patrick's Day, Chente helped Vitalino make a large, red, triangular kite with long, sparkly side fringes, some green, some gold, and two long green and sparkly tails, making the kite look like a beautiful quetzal bird in flight.

Before taking his kite and rapidly heading to the kite flying competition, Vitalino took one last quick peek out of the kitchen window of his home toward the sowing fields, trying to tell Chente apart from the other men coming on the trail. However, they still were too far away; they still looked like rag dolls.

It will take them about an hour to get here, he thought. That would give him enough time to fly his kite, win a prize, and still have time to be outside the church to help Chente with the firecrackers and fireworks brought by the priest to be lit up before Mass.

The village was too small and too poor to have its own priest, so a priest from the nearest town came on horseback the last Sunday of every month. It was a three-hour journey that usually began at five o'clock in the morning.

The priest usually spent only the necessary time in the village. He rushed to visit the sick and quickly blessed the dying. That done, walking at a fast pace, he reached the town's outskirts, where he hastily got on a high-spirited horse and was off at full gallop.

The people who usually walked with the priest to the edge of the village to see him off stood there the forty minutes it took him to get gradually smaller and smaller, and finally disappeared in the distance.

That tragic St Patrick's Day, the priest arrived at the church around two o'clock. Because that was a special day, two young, indigenous priests fresh out of the seminary came with him.

That day was a pleasant surprise for the villagers, because they never dreamed that in that small church, the walls of which were made of adobe and a thatch roof and in the middle of an insignificant village, would someday have three priests celebrating Mass.

The Mass that day for the villagers was truly solemn, filling their hearts with intense devotion and fulfilling their spiritual needs. The three priests sang in Latin, and as soon as they finished the blessing of the whole village, the older priest ended the holy Mass.

It was only five in the afternoon, but the fog and the shadows of the mountains had swallowed the village whole. The people lit up the small park with oil lamps and torches for lack of electricity.

The villagers arranged the pine tables of every home and set them in the brightest spot of the park and decorated them with clay jugs full of brightly colored flowers and fragrant herbs and leaves.

When the three priests arrived at the dinner table hand in hand with the children, they were received joyfully by the men and women. The women served traditional appetizers of the region right away, leaving the main course for last—the village's pride, iguana stew. The dinosaurs may have ruled the earth for millions of years but some of their descendants ended up in a humble earthen pot.

Dinner finished, the boys and girls stood facing the dinner table in an orderly fashion, keeping enough distance between them and the table so that they could dance freely.

All the kids put on ancient masks handed down from generation to generation. Some depicted the suffering and pain, others the terror of the massacres of the Spanish conquest.

The musicians stood behind the kids, some with big old wood and leather drums, others with bamboo flutes. Five big old drums resounded in the stillness of the night for five minutes. When the drums suddenly stopped, the flute's sad melody was heard, which was the cue for the kids to begin dancing. And dancing with the gracefulness and talent of Russian dancers were the children, when a burst of machine gunfire compelled an overwhelming silence upon the entire village—a cemetery silence with a stench of dead flowers.

Only when the village fell silent did the villagers pay attention to the loud sounds of cicadas and crickets, who had been futilely trying to warn them of the imminent danger. Out of the fog came the soldiers like a nightmare that had just become a reality.

The platoon leader was a burly man. He approached the dinner table, gun in hand, grabbed the earthen jug that contained the diluted chicha, and drank greedily. He let the fermented liquid mixed with water and sugar run down from the corners of his lips, wetting his throat and chest.

As soon as he had his fill of chicha, the man pulled one of the tablecloths, throwing to the ground everything that was on it, and then he tried to dry his throat and chest while glaring at the three priests.

"What an excellent rebel camp you have here. I am sure you are training them properly." The voice of the platoon leader resounded in the stillness of the night like a big old drum.

The terror those soldiers represented had accelerated the villagers' hearts, but to hear the platoon leader speak those terrifying words numbed their senses because they knew those words meant a death sentence.

The priest in charge, a tall fifty-year-old with a head full of gray hair, got up from his seat and in six long strides approached the platoon leader and said in a firm tone of voice, "Good evening, Lieutenant, may God bless you and your men. Let me assure you that what we have here is not what it appears to be. These are good-hearted people and good Christians. Tonight, we are celebrating St…"

One of the lieutenant's bullets stopped him from finishing his sentence.

The priest's head hit the edge of one of the tables when he fell to the ground, but he felt no pain because he was already dead.

Sheer panic spread like wildfire among the villagers, some of the kids crying and some screaming as they ran to the open arms of their parents, while a couple of the older kids managed to run away and escape.

The platoon leader shot six bullets into the air, trying to make the villagers stop screaming. The villagers, completely terrified, screamed louder.

With his vision blurred by his tears, Vitalino looked for his mother among the people gathering around the young priests trying to find protection in them. But the poor young priests were so terrified that they dared not move from their seats, and with abundant tears streaming down their pale cheeks were repeating over and over, "Holy Mary mother of God, pray for us sinners, now and at the hour of our death. Amen."

Vitalino found his father facing the priest's table on his knees and saying the Hail Mary with them.

"Chente!" shouted Vitalino as he hugged his father from behind. Chente pulled him over his shoulder and made him roll on the ground and under the table where a pair of hands grabbed him. Vitalino turned around and hugged Tomasita, his mother.

"Who is the mayor of this wretched village?" the lieutenant repeatedly shouted. An extraordinarily skinny and tiny little man who looked like a small boy was approaching the lieutenant very slowly.

That little man was dressed in black from head to toe and could have easily been mistaken for the big hat, a character in one of Guatemala's myths and legends.

The tiny man said something to the lieutenant in a feeble, trembling voice. "I can't hear a word you are saying. Speak like a man!" shouted the lieutenant. The little man, making an extraordinary effort, raised his voice to the fifth power and said, "We don't have a mayor."

The lieutenant watched the tiny man with an amused expression and mockingly said, "You do not have to shout at me, you tiny son of a female Chihuahuan." The lieutenant found that extremely funny and burst out laughing. The lieutenant's laughter sounded like it was coming from a metal drum, like those drums used by musicians in Trinidad and Tobago.

When the lieutenant stopped laughing, he asked the wee man his name. "Pablito, the milkman," said the tiny man.

"Pablito the milkman," repeated the lieutenant and again exploded in laughter.

Pablito mistakenly took that as a good sign and gave the lieutenant his best smile, showing him his superior gum, a thick and broad toothless gum that looked like it was that of a chimpanzee.

It was easier for Pablito to encounter a traveler from a distant galaxy than to see a dentist in that god-forsaken village.

Pablito's toothless gum made the lieutenant laugh so hard that when he finally stopped laughing, he said to Pablito with eyes full of tears, "Well, my gummy friend, tonight is your lucky night. By the powers invested in me, I name you the first mayor of this metropolis. Your first task as mayor will be to shut your people up."

Pablito went to talk to his people, and minutes later, the lieutenant could only hear one or two muffled sobs. "That is much better," said the lieutenant loudly. He was going to continue talking but stopped when he saw the people gathered around the newly named mayor, and he wondered what they were saying to him.

Patience was not one of the lieutenant's qualities, but curiosity got the better of him, and oddly enough, he decided to wait.

Pablito the milkman, as his people called him, had taken his role as mayor seriously. When his people finished telling him the message, they wanted him to convey, he turned around with great resolve to go to the spot where the lieutenant was waiting.

Before Pablito could take the first step in the direction of the lieutenant, one of the young priests grabbed him by his right arm and kneeled on the ground to talk to him as if the newly named mayor was a little child.

"Please, sir, I beg you to stay here and pray with us, do not talk to that man, please. He is an evil man and will surely kill you."

What little patience the lieutenant fleetingly showed the villagers was long gone. "Release the honorable mayor of pathetic village," he shouted at the young priest. The young priest let go of Pablito's arm as if it was on fire.

As Pablito was bravely approaching the spot where the lieutenant was waiting, the lieutenant watched him with the same kind of curiosity with which a cat watches a mouse in a barn.

Pablito did not speak Spanish and had to make a tremendous effort to translate his language into Spanish at the same time he was talking. Still, he managed to communicate the wishes of his people to the lieutenant, even though his Spanish came out twisted and upside down.

It went something like this. "Sir, Mister Lieutenant, you, the people's villagers of this village, want and wish to remind you to remember you, your person yourself, of the rights of humans, the right to live. Me, my person, myself as mayor authority of this village, named by your person, you your own self, order you to please them, the peoples, and to go out and leave together with your men." Then he added, "Please."

The laughter of the lieutenant and his men shattered the stillness of the cold night like an explosion.

When the lieutenant and his men stopped laughing, he took advantage of the confusion and silence of the villagers and shouted for everyone to hear: "We have reliable information that you people are collaborators of the Communists in this area. My men will interrogate every one of you, but not to worry, my men are professionals who have graduated from the best universities. Said the man sarcastically. They will do what they must do subtly and humanely."

Among the confusion, the cries, and screams, a woman with a baby in her arms shouted, "Those Communists come down from the mountain and force us to give them food!" But no one heard her.

The soldiers took the villagers to the church, interrogated them, and then killed them. And to make sure they were dead, the soldiers threw hand grenades on top of the heap of bodies.

The soldiers set the church and the village on fire. Vitalino and his mother miraculously escaped by jumping into the darkness of one of the town's steep slopes. They landed on soft, loose ground and went tumbling and rolling down the hill.

Every time they stopped rolling, they got up and tried to walk in complete darkness, only to fall and roll down the slope again.

Vitalino and his mother were bleeding from their painful injuries, but when Vitalino heard the river's quiet singing, he knew they were safe. He took his mother's hand in total darkness and led her to the river with only the stars' light to help.

Vitalino and his mother waded in the cold and waist-deep water and followed the river. When they came to a spot where two giant boulders were choking the river, making it narrower, deeper, and faster, Vitalino said to his mother, "Carry me, Mom, it is too deep for me."

Tomasita went around one of the boulders carrying Vitalino on her back while the water came up to her chin.

As Tomasita advanced around the big rock, the water level descended. When she got out of the river, the water only reached up to her ankles.

Tomasita lowered her son in the shallow water and immediately began feeling her way in complete darkness, trying to get her bearings in that cold and dark place. When she blindly felt her way around and discovered that she was between the big rock and the rocky bottom of the hill with no way out, she fell to her knees, totally exhausted and disheartened.

Tomasita had begun the previous day around four o'clock in the morning, and by looking at the position of the stars, she knew it was around four o'clock the following day.

The terrifying events the soldiers brought, together with the incredible weariness and cold that were biting her body and soul, were all taking a heavy toll on her body and mind. Suddenly, Tomasita's brain began offering her terrifying thoughts.

"What if that boy in the dark with you whose breathing you can hear but he you cannot see isn't really your son but an evil spirit? One of those evil spirits that is always prowling around the hills of the village ready to take people with evil incantations to dark and cold places, like the one you are at now." Would it reveal its real self before killing you?"

"Don't you know about all those men, women, and children who vanish from the village without a trace? Yes, you do." *But I never let go of my boy's hand from the moment we came out from under the table where we were hiding,* she thought. *Or did I? Yes, I did, every time we stumbled and fell in that pitch darkness where I could not even see my hands in front of my eyes. Yet the boy always found me, helped me up and, taking my hand, guided me to the river.* She kept thinking, *Perhaps Vitalino cracked his head on a rock and is lying dead on the hill? Maybe this evil creature took his voice and his place.*

"Don't be afraid. We are almost there." The voice of the boy pounced into her thoughts.

"Where are you taking me?" she yelled at him, trembling in fear. "You maleficent demon! You can kill me, but you can't take my soul," she cried in despair.

"Don't be afraid," repeated the boy while taking her hand and leading her to a narrow and low tunnel at water's level.

"We will have to go on our hands and knees. Keep your chin in the water so you do not hit your head on the rocks." Tomasita was all out of energy and willpower, so she just followed the kid's voice for a seemingly endless twenty meters in pitch darkness and on hands and knees.

When they finally reached a sandy patch, the boy helped her stand up and guided her to a rocky wall. "Keep both your hands on the wall and walk close to it, and do not let go of the wall, or you will fall into the abyss."

"What abyss?" Tomasita wanted to ask, but her voice was long gone.

Tomasita clung to the rocky wall, which was wet and cold. But the water in the tunnel was colder, so she did not notice it. They walked close to the wall for some twenty paces. When the wall veered to the left, they found themselves in a giant dome chamber, dimly lit by the light of a large bonfire burning happily some twenty meters farther inside the cavern.

When Tomasita finally saw her son's face in the dim light, she hugged and kissed him with loads of tears running down her cheeks. When she finished wiping her tears away, she looked in the direction of the bonfire and saw three people sitting around the reassuring fire.

"Who are those people?" she asked Vitalino in a low voice.

"Only Chente and I knew of this place. That must be his spirit because he is already dead," Vitalino said while silently crying. Vitalino's words reminded Tomasita that when they were about to get in the river, they heard the gunshots and the explosion of the hand grenades.

"Chente! Chente!" Tomasita screamed. The three people sitting around the fire got up and ran toward Tomasita and her son. Vitalino and his mother could not believe their eyes. There was Chente, Katocha, and Tono of the village. The five of them melted into a single body and a single crying.

The five survivors walked to the bonfire, where they sat around it and talked and cried for a long time, and when they ran out of tears, they fell asleep.

They slept all day, but before the sun sank behind the mountains, Chente and Tono climbed up some vines and roots that hung from a narrow gap on the dome ceiling. When they were sure there were no soldiers around, they got out through the opening and gathered wood for the fire. Meanwhile, Tomasita, Katocha, and Vitalino gathered many crabs, which were easy pickings because the cave floor and walls were crawling with them.

When the new fire lit up the cave, and the sweet smell of barbecued crabs permeated the air, the five survivors sat down to eat. And while they ate, Chente told how he and Katocha had survived the village massacre.

"When the soldiers began firing their guns, the people ran in terror to the rear of the church where Katocha and I were standing. Many dead and some wounded fell on us, protecting us from the bullets. When the soldiers set the church on fire, we managed to escape through a window and fled to the river, and there we ran into Tono."

"I was coming back from visiting my youngest sister who had been ill for some time," said Tono. "When I was approaching the village's fringe, I saw it on fire. I ran to see what had happened, but when I saw the soldiers, I too fled to the river."

Day and night, the five survivors talked about the events of that tragic night, until they ran out of words, and silence became the lord of the cave once more.

The five of them tried unsuccessfully to steer their thoughts in another direction, but when they least expected, there came at full speed the unstoppable train of the memories of that tragic night to hit them and dragged them along with it.

On the third day, the survivors woke up physically sore and mentally devastated but with their survival instinct wide awake. "We've got to get out of here," said Chente. "We must get into the jungle and get to a place where they will never find us."

"All we must do is to follow the river to its source." Everyone agreed with Chente.

"After all," said Tono, "there is not a crab left in the cave."

Before they left the safety of the cave, Tono, who was the only one of them who knew how to read and write Spanish, read to them a message he had written on the wall closest to the opening on the dome ceiling.

HERE WERE KATOCHA COY, TONO KAAL, TOMASITA, CHENTE, AND VITALINO TAHUITE. ONLY SURVIVORS OF THE MASSACRE OF THE VILLAGE OF SAINT PATRICK. MAY GOD HAVE MERCY ON US.

***

When Vitalino returned from his short trip down memory lane, which only lasted a few thousandths of a second, he saw Mariano on the floor gaping at him as if Vitalino was just coming out of a parallel universe. When he recognized his old drill instructor wearing a soldier's uniform, he and his two men saluted him military style, then went to help him get up from the ground.

"What happened here, sir?" asked Vitalino, looking Mariano straight in the eye to see if he was telling the truth. Mariano looked at Vitalino and said, "These criminals tried to kill me. If it weren't for my dogs, I would be dead." Vitalino did not swallow Mariano's story, but he had not the slightest interest in finding the truth, so he just let it go.

The ambulances took the injured gang members to the hospital. Ambulances for dogs were non-existent, so the policemen helped Mariano take the wounded and the dead dogs to his pickup truck. He thanked the policemen and hurriedly wanted to shake hands with them, but they insisted on saluting Vitalino's former drill instructor military style.

While the policemen saluted him, Mariano thought that belonging to the Guatemalan army was a blessing. He got in his pickup truck and was gone.

The reporters and the rescue squad chief gathered around Vitalino to hear his explanation of the killings of young men and dogs. Vitalino was, after all, the barrio's chief of police, so he did what most police officers in Guatemala do with ease when they want to get out of a tight spot—fabricate a story.

No one questioned Vitalino's explanation of the events that had taken place there. After all, they were only street gang members and a bunch of street dogs.

DOG OF LITTLE FAITH

———————

When Bella came to, she sprang up and ran around the battleground dazed and confused. Something deep inside her was telling her to look for her babies, but she did not remember what they looked like or what they were. She was unable to think, remember or behave in a normal way. She stopped running and sat on the ground in a catatonic, stupor-like state, her nose bleeding and her mouth slobbering.

Every time Bella came out of that pitiful state, she ran around the battlefield and then suddenly stopped, only to fall into that sorry state again. Three gang members had attacked her with aluminum bats, but when they were about to finish her off, Mariano's gunshots sent them scattering. Mariano had unknowingly saved her life.

Pepita and Cinderella found Bella. They threw themselves to the ground close to Bella's feet, exhausted. Pepita had only minor injuries, and Cinderella limped from one of her rear legs; other than that, they were okay.

The girls had not rested a minute when suddenly Bella sprang up and was gone. Cinderella and Pepita caught up at Bella's next stop and threw themselves to the ground, only to spring up and run after her again.

After running and stopping for an endless twenty minutes, the girls realized something was wrong with Bella. Making a tremendous effort, they guided her home, which was a frustrating effort. Every time they came close to the ravine's edge, Bella went running and stopping again and again.

When the dead tired girls finally managed to get her home, they found Ronaldinho lying outside the cave. He had a nasty, long, deep machete wound on his back that would not stop bleeding. While Cinderella tried to heal him, Pepita managed to get Bella into the cave.

Inside the cave, Pepita found Fortunato resting his head on Alexander's dead body. All Pepita could see in Fortunato's open eyes was profound sadness. Alexander had fought like a warrior and had died too young.

Pepita left Bella sitting with her sight lost on one of the walls and went to hug Fortunato and Alexander.

A couple of hours later, Mariano came looking for some of his injured friends. Cindy had gone with the dead and injured dogs in the pickup truck, thanks to her lucky star she was not injured when the thugs attacked her family. She came back with Mariano and the veterinarian who always cared for Mariano's dogs. The veterinarian came with her assistant, a young man who carried a leather first aid bag.

When Pepita and Fortunato heard the voices of Mariano and his companions, they got out of the cave, and after greeting Cindy and Mariano, they went to sniff the newcomers. The newcomers had never dealt with street dogs before and were so afraid that they dared not move, not even a finger.

With Mariano and the vet assistant's help, the veterinarian did everything she could to help the dog's injuries. And then she said to Mariano that if he wanted to save Ronaldinho's life, they would have to take him to intensive care at once.

Mariano quickly did what he needed to do; remembering his days as a soldier, he dropped to the ground and crawled into the cave. Once inside, he asked the vet's assistant to hand him the box of sausages, the gallon of water, and the plastic bowl he had brought for the dogs.

While his friends ate, he tried to take Bella out of the cave, but every time he came close to her, she showed him her fangs while growling threateningly. Mariano left her and took Alexander's dead body as he crawled out of the cave.

While Mariano described Bella's condition to the vet, her assistant placed Alexander's body in a black plastic bag. The vet quickly fixed an injection and explained to Mariano how and where to give it to Bella. While Mariano crawled back into the cave, the vet and her assistant began the climb out of the ravine, ending an adventure she would talk about the rest of her life.

With Cinderella's help, Mariano gave Bella the shot, then he gave a quick look at the dogs and felt satisfied with what he had done for them. He then said goodbye and rapidly crawled out of the cave, but not before taking a few fleas with him.

Once outside, Mariano lifted Ronaldinho from the ground and carried him in his arms to the highway where he had left his vehicle, Cindy and Cinderella led the way uphill. When Mariano reached the pickup, those two were already waiting for him.

Mariano placed Ronaldinho carefully in one of the padded cages, Cindy and Cinderella got in the other one next to their brother. Mariano locked the cages and rushed to the vet's clinic, not wanting to waste another minute.

With Ronaldinho on his mind, Mariano failed to notice the eerie silence and the weird fact that no vehicles were going in any direction on that usually busy highway.

They had not traveled along the highway for a minute when suddenly Cindy exclaimed in great amazement, "Look, Cinderella, look!" while pointing with her nose at a gorgeous looking dog running alongside the pickup without making the slightest effort. The dog appeared to be flying, because his feet did not seem to touch the pavement.

The handsome devil of the highway was as beautiful as he was charming. When he realized that the girls were admiring him, he bowed his head and pretended to take off an imaginary hat in the style of yesteryear's gentlemen.

"Hi there, gorgeous!" said Cinderella in a Madrid accent.

"Where are you going, little rabbit?" said Cindy.

"Oh dear, oh dear, I shall be too late," said Guapo, stealing a few words from *Alice in Wonderland* while jumping on the pickup as effortlessly as if he could fly.

Once on the pickup, he approached the girls' cage, got his head through the mesh as if it was not there, and kissed the girls on the mouth, leaving them stunned and gaping. Guapo then approached Ronaldinho's cage.

Guapo took one look at Ronaldinho and said in a commanding tone of voice: "Get up and walk." With a voice so weak that it was almost inaudible, Ronaldinho said to Guapo, "I would if I could, but right now, I can't even wag my tail, let alone walk through that mesh."

"Canine of little faith thou art, don't you know that if you had faith the size of a grain of mustard seed, you could move mountains?"

"How wonderful life would be if what you say were true, but I have never heard anyone say: 'see those mountains on the horizon, they used to be right here. I moved them with my faith.'"

A bit annoyed, Guapo said to Ronaldinho, "When I say mountains, I…" Poof! He vanished into thin air. Mariano had taken the first exit out of the highway and out of Guapo's territory.

"I guess we will never know what he meant by mountains, huh?" said Cindy. But Cinderella did not hear her. She was seeing the golden thread that had always united her to Ronaldinho slowly disappearing, and she knew then that Ronaldinho was dying.

"Ronaldinho, my soul!" Cinderella cried out, and her entire being went out of her in that cry.

Ronaldinho and Cinderella had been inseparable since the day they were born. When the deceased boozer snatched them from their lair, Ronaldinho held her trembling body close to his, reassuring her, telling her not to worry and that everything would be fine. She found comfort in his words even though she could feel fear in his little heart.

During Mariano's rough and demanding training, when she lost her first fight on a Saturday afternoon, Ronaldinho was always there to comfort her and put a smile back in her heart. Now he was dead, and a part of her died with him.

Cinderella and Cindy cried and howled so loudly that Mariano had to stop at the side of the road. When he got to the rear of his vehicle, he already knew Ronaldinho was dead.

Mariano took his dead friend out of the cage, held him close to his heart, and rocked him as if he was a newborn baby while crying and howling as loudly and with as much sadness as Cindy and Cinderella.

The veterinarian had stopped behind Mariano's pickup truck, and when she saw the way Mariano was behaving, she looked at her assistant, who was staring and gaping at Mariano. She poked him with her elbow, and when he looked at her, she pointed her index finger at her right temple and twisted it in a circular motion while crossing her eyes and sticking her tongue out and to one side of her mouth.

THE CUBAN BLACK WOMAN

———◆———

Eight weeks had passed after the great battle between the dogs and the street gang. Bella was still disoriented even though she did not look as haggard as the first days. She still walked around looking for her pups but not as desperately as before. Most of her time she spent staring at one of the walls in the cave with her ever-present drool hanging from her mouth.

Pepita and Fortunato had taken good care of Bella all that time she was oblivious of life around her. Pepita and Fortunato walked with her and made sure she ate and drank enough water.

Thanks to Mariano's twice-weekly visits, food had been easily obtainable. He always brought with him plenty of food and water. He usually brought leftovers, food from the pet store, and sausages as well. If he did not find them in the cave, he just pushed everything in the cave and left.

On Christmas Eve, around noon, Pepita, Bella, and Fortunato arrived at Pepita's lair after spending a few days in the forest. When they entered the cave, they were surprised to find it cheerfully illuminated by some

Christmas little lights flashing merrily thanks to the energy provided by a car's battery. Part of the ground was covered with Christmas wrapping paper, and on it were all kinds of dog treats.

As soon as Pepita finished eating, she approached Fortunato; she kissed him and licked his face tenderly, and then she lovingly nibbled his ears. Fortunato enjoyed Pepita's caressing but felt that there was something terribly strange in her behavior. Suddenly his body shook violently as if an electrical current was coursing through it. When he stopped shaking, he was left there stunned and gasping for air.

Before Fortunato had time to recover from that state of shock, he sensed that something frightening was about to happen, and that made his hair stand on end, and a strong smell of fear emanated from his body.

Unable to comprehend what his eyes were showing him, Fortunato saw Guapo get into the cave through one of the walls in his most putrid and horrifying form and emitting a rotten smell. That hellish vision left Fortunato in a deep stupor.

Pepita went to the spot where Bella was staring at one of the walls and unceremoniously kissed her on the mouth. She then licked Bella's mouth and swallowed the thick and slimy saliva hanging from Bella's half-open mouth. That done, she turned around, walked through Guapo's body, unaware of his presence, and went out of the cave with a male dog in mind.

Guapo approached Bella and licked her ears while whispering, "Wake up Bella, wake up." That said, he turned around and fixed his eyes on Fortunato and in a resounding voice said to him, "I would like to stay and talk awhile, but I have a rendezvous on the highway." That said, he disappeared, but not his fetid stench.

Guapo's stench, mixed with Fortunato's smell of fear, penetrated Bella's olfactory system like a thunderbolt, and that shook her out of her semi-catatonic state. When she stopped shaking, she looked around with her eyes wide open and fully conscious of herself. Suddenly it dawned on her that she just came out of a realm of darkness and hopelessness.

Taking a deep breath, Bella tried to swallow life through her nose and tried to absorb her world through her eyes. Bella became aware of Fortunato's stupor state and reacted instinctively. With all her strength, she pushed Fortunato, and he went rolling violently. That push made him get back to the world of the living as if Bella's hard shove had pulled his legs out of a high voltage trap. Even with his eyes wide open and all his senses in full alert, Fortunato could not believe his eyes; there was Bella alive, her tail wagging, and she was back to her old self again.

"If you want to see Pepita one last time, we better hurry up," Bella said to Fortunato as naturally as if she had never been in a semi-catatonic state. They ran out of the cave, and once outside, they looked up at the top of the steep hill, and the last thing they saw of Pepita was her tail leaving the edge of the ravine. They ran up the slope, but they could not find Pepita anywhere when they reached the summit.

"Mom," said Fortunato in a shaky voice, stuttering and trying very hard not to cry, "where is Pep-Pepita go-going?"

Bella saw a mixture of fear and sadness in Fortunato's face, so she pounced on him playfully and while hugging him, she said in the heavy and husky accent of a negro Cuban woman, which surprised her as much as it did Fortunato, "Aah, baby! Time flies, you know. When you least think about her, when you least expect it, she will be back among us."

"She will?" asked Fortunato with his shaky voice.

"Of course, baby, she always is."

Bella kept talking in a Cuban woman's accent, trying to get Pepita out of Fortunato's mind. "You know, baby, we have not been to the forest in a long time; we must go and chase them ducks, they must be too fat for lack of exercise."

"But we just got here from the forest," protested Fortunato.

"What I tell you? Time flies, we just got here from the woods, and it already feels like we have not been there in a long time," responded Bella with clarity. And then she said, "I bet you a bone I get to the small pond before you." That said, she went quickly downhill with a big smile in her eyes, followed by Fortunato, whose heart was bursting with joy.

BEETHOVEN'S 5TH SYMPHONY

ll that time that Bella was out of reality, Pepita had spent all her free time showing Fortunato every nook and cranny of the forest and the ravine. Pepita showed him the best spots to fish and hunt and was also her instructor in the fine art of finding and eating food scraps in the garbage dump.

Pepita taught Fortunato not to disdain the contents of disposable diapers as well. Thanks to Pepita's teachings, Fortunato became the master of the forest, the ravine, and the garbage dump.

A warm afternoon several weeks after being abandoned by Pepita, Fortunato had a big fat possum cornered in some bushes. He did not want to catch it; he only wanted to play with it. Fortunato jumped and pounced, barking playfully, unaware of three pairs of eyes watching him. Three slender bodies stealthily drawing nearer in the tall grass had him in their eyesight. When they were at the proper distance, they jumped simultaneously on Fortunato, sending him rolling on the ground. Fortunato sprang up startled and ran at full speed, not looking back at his attackers, just hoping to make it to Bella's protection.

Fortunato's pursuers were snapping at his rear legs, trying to bring him down. When he felt he was a goner, he saw Bella, Lucky, and Cinderella running toward him. That gave him the courage to stop running and face his attackers, but the moment he stopped running, he was hit and run over by his pursuers. And again, he went rolling on the ground. When Fortunato managed to get up, he found himself face to face with Cindy, Anaximenes, and Anaximander.

The surprise and the overwhelming happiness were too much for Fortunato, and he tried to run away, but Cindy, Anaximenes, and Anaximander pinned him to the ground.

With his head between the legs of Anaximenes and Anaximander, Fortunato saw Peregrino coming toward him. Peregrino had not been restored to his full health. He was walking slowly and rhythmically, moving his whole body as if walking to the beat of Beethoven's 5th Symphony, and every two steps, he threw his head to one side and then up.

Peregrino slowly made it to the spot where his family was waiting for him, and they all hugged and kissed for a long while. When they had enough love and affection, they all walked pleasantly in the woods to the cadence of the music that only Peregrino could hear, and that was when Fortunato asked the questions no one wanted to hear.

"Where are my brothers and sisters?" he said, his voice breaking. "Where are Ronaldinho and Pirate?" No one wanted to answer those questions.

Following a short silence that seemed to them like an eternity, Peregrino, with a lump in his throat, said quietly, "We are the only survivors of the massacre, and you should be happy to be alive. You should be proud because you fought like a great warrior and risked your life to protect little Alexander. Ronaldinho, Pirate, Dawn, Pure, Niño, Hayfield, Eros, and Alexander are now among the stars."

The family walked back to their lair silently and with heavy hearts. The loss of their loved ones was a tremendous pain to bear, especially for the young ones.

When they got to their lair, Cinderella saw Fortunato devastated, so she tried to cheer him up by saying, "the good news is that we all are going to live at Mariano's house. It all depends on you, if you want to come, we will live happily ever after."

Pirate had been Fortunato's hero, his idol, the one member of his family he admired the most. "What will happen to our treasures after we are gone? The ravine, the forest, the garbage dump, and the cave?" Asked Fortunato.

"Others will come, others will cherish them," said Cinderella.

"Thanks, but no thanks," said Fortunato with a lump in his throat. "I wouldn't abandon my world to go to Mariano's world even if I knew the ravine, the garbage dump, and the forest would explode in tiny pieces. I wouldn't change the gorge, the garbage dump, and the forest, not even for a hundred Marianos." That said, Fortunato howled mournfully, trying to get all the grief out of his heart, and the whole clan howled with him.

MOONSHINE AND MAXIMÓN (A MAYAN PAGAN IDOL)

———————

M ariano, not wanting to follow the dogs through the garbage dump when they went looking for Pepita, Bella, and Fortunato, went down the ravine through Pepita's shortcut. He had no doubt they had a secret retreat in that vast ravine, and he was resolved to find it.

When Mariano arrived at the semi-vertical wall that was part of Pepita's shortcut, he thought that it would not be possible for him to continue descending. But thanks to his army training, he was the kind of man who achieved whatever task he determined to do.

This drop is a minor obstacle for a soldier, he thought. And right away he remembered the long rope under his double cab pickup's rear seat. That rope he knew would be long enough to take him to the bottom of the semi-vertical wall. And he began climbing the steep slope toward the edge of the highway where he left his vehicle.

Mariano returned to the semi-vertical wall carrying the rope and right away secured one end to the nearest tree and he began descending to the wall's bottom.

As soon as he got his feet on the ground, Mariano began the search for his friends. He looked everywhere but found nothing. He searched in every nook and cranny of the enormous ravine but could find neither hide nor hair of his friends.

He came to stand facing the three walls that made up the garbage dam, and again he thought there was nowhere else to go. He whistled loudly while walking all over the humongous ravine, wishing his friends would answer his call, but nothing. Mariano pulled his gun out of its holster, and he fired five shots in different directions, but nothing happened.

Tiredness made Mariano look at his wristwatch, and it reminded him that he had been looking for his friends for several hours, so he sat on the ground to take a short rest. It was then that he saw the dog tracks printed lightly on the rocky floor. Mariano jumped up and followed the footprints to the mound in the shape of a tiny volcano that had formed there by the mud, debris, rocks, and the limbs of the trees dragged there by the last landslide.

Mariano climbed the small volcano and found the hole shaped like a volcano's crater, which Bella had dug up to find a way out. The hole was covered with dog's hair, Mariano noticed. And that made him smile, happy to have found his friends' entrance to their secret retreat.

On his hands and knees, Mariano stuck his head into the hole, but all he could see was a dark and narrow tunnel. With his head in the crater, he whistled several times, but only the echo whistled back at him. Mariano kicked the edges of the hole to get more sunlight in there so he could have a better look, but the mixture of mud, rocks, and debris would not budge.

Half the solar disc had sunk on the horizon. The enormous ravine's edges and several meters down still had plenty of sunlight, but in the bottom of it, the light was hightailing it out of there.

The dark tunnel had captured Mariano's imagination; he was sure his friends were somewhere inside, and he did not want to leave without first surprising his friends in their secret hideout.

With the energy of a stubborn man, Mariano tried to enlarge the hole by hitting the edges with all his might, utilizing the thick and heavy tree branch he found lying there on the ground; but to no avail, the mixture of mud and debris was petrified.

When Mariano was determined to do something, he invariably achieved it, which was his best asset, but occasionally it was his downfall. When he realized that darkness was creeping on him, he remembered where he was and got mad at himself for letting it surprise him so foolishly.

Mariano knew that he had to get out of the ravine real fast, or he would have to share the night with the night residents of the gorge, mainly the poisonous snakes which he loathed with his entire being.

He knew he was in a place where one could break a leg or two in broad daylight, and at night, it was perilous, so he had no other choice but to crawl to the semi-vertical wall in pitch darkness.

It was well into the night when Mariano managed to get to the spot on the highway where he had left his vehicle. He had bruises, scrapes, and bumps all over his body. Even though he could not feel his knees, he knew they were bleeding.

The last two hundred meters to the slope's summit, he climbed on his hands and knees, and thanks to the steepness of the hill, several times he went rolling downhill to the spot where he had started.

In one of those times that he rolled downhill, he hit his head on the edge of a big rock and was knocked unconscious. Three hours after waking up from the rock's induced sleep, Mariano arrived at his vehicle, or at least, to what was left of it.

Mariano's ears were buzzing as if a thousand ravines' mosquitos had gotten in his head through the big cut in his scalp the edge of the rock had opened. His brain was throbbing, and so was his entire skull. On top of all that, he had the strange feeling that part of his brain was melted on his shoulders as if it were hot lasagna with extra cheese.

Suddenly, everything began spinning around him. He bent forward, spread his legs, and held his knees to steady himself. Then, effortlessly and without thinking twice about it, he vomited fluidly and plentifully.

When Mariano's stomach was empty, it heaved a few times, and then he just stood there, stunned and in a load of pain. The terrible pain and the vomiting forced Mariano to vividly remember every detail of the incident at Purgatory. Purgatory was a small indigenous village where he had gone to beg Maximón, a Mayan pagan idol that has been around for centuries, to silence the voice of his conscience. A wooden effigy dressed up sometimes as a cowboy, sometimes as a soldier or a businessman, it is a saint that answers prayers for good or evil purposes, also known as grandfather.

Mariano's conscience was screaming at him for all the people he had killed when he was a lieutenant in the army during the Guatemalan internal armed conflict. And every scream of his conscience was like a hammer's blow to his brain and eardrums.

Mariano's brain and eardrums were in unbearable, throbbing pain, driving him entirely out of his mind. So, he wasted no time with good manners to the people lining up outside the temple waiting for the shaman to let them in. He just fired three shots in the air and everyone there, including the shaman, scampered away.

On his knees at the feet of Maximón, Mariano opened a bottle of Guatemala's High lands moonshine and lit up two fine cigars. He stuck a lit cigar in the half open mouth of Maximón and while he drank and smoked, he poured moonshine on Maximón's feet.

Mariano implored Maximón to stop the pounding in his head and eardrums and begged for forgiveness for his mortal sins. As soon as the bottle of moonshine was empty and the cigars smoked, the screams of his conscience gradually turned into muffled whispers.

Mariano opened a second bottle of moonshine and lit two aromatic cigars which perfumed the small temple. When the second bottle was half empty, Mariano heard Maximón speak to him in a fatherly voice: "I will take your pain away, son, but your mortal sins you shall wash out with your blood and loads of pain and sorrow, but I will make sure you do not die of it.

By the time the second bottle of moonshine was empty, and there were not even the ashes left of the aromatic cigars, with considerable difficulty and leaning on Maximón's knees, Mariano got up from the cold dirt floor where he had been sitting at Maximón's feet, who was life-sized and clad in a black suit and white hat at that shrine.

Once up, Mariano tried to steady himself and, making a tremendous effort, placed one of the guns he was carrying in each shoulder holster at Maximón's lap.

His tongue swollen and his mouth numbed because of the side effects of the extra virgin moonshine, he said in a drunken voice and with a grimace that turned his face into a facial expression of excruciating pain, "Thank you, thank you, Grandpa, thank you, Grandpa."

Mariano took a few faltering steps and then, staggering, managed to get out of the sacred temple of Maximón.

Once outside the temple, the whole village began spinning around him in an astonishingly fast motion. He bent forward, spread his legs, and held his knees to steady himself, and then vomited as fluidly and as plentifully as he had just done it by the side of the highway where he had left his vehicle.

When Mariano stopped vomiting, he was not in the mood to accept the fact that his car had been turned into junk by some gang members to avenge the deaths of their mates.

Thanks to the highway's lights and the vehicle's lights passing by, he could see the damage done to his car. The windows were all smashed in, the upholstery completely ripped, and many parts of the car torn to pieces. The four tires were gone, and there was nothing left of the front and rear lights.

Along the pickup's right side, someone had written with a sharp metal object in big capital letters, and between parentheses, "MURDERER CHAFAROTE." Chafarote is the denigrating nickname Guatemalans give to military personal of any rank.

As Mariano drew his 9mm pistol, the lights of the passing cars shone on a short message written on the gun barrel in silver and raised letters that said, "Free Body Piercing."

Mariano walked along the edge of the highway looking for gang members or anyone who looked like a thug, to give them a taste of his justice; so that he could assuage his thirst for revenge. That thirst for revenge was eating away at his mind, soul, and even his socks, as if it were sulfuric acid. Unfortunately for Mariano, there was not a soul anywhere.

The whole place seemed deserted, but Mariano knew that mocking eyes were looking at him under cover of darkness among some abandoned houses on the other side of the highway.

Mariano was walking back to his wrecked car when out of the abandoned houses on the other side of the highway came the loud and clear whistle that civilians in Guatemala whistle to pick a fight with military men. Mariano climbed up the hillock that was by the highway's edge and, aiming his gun at the abandoned houses, fired a barrage of bullets. He reloaded and fired again till the magazine was empty.

Mariano's gunshots' staccato traveled in the echo's vocal cords to the neighborhood. It reached a couple of drug dealers' ears, who were sitting on the trunk of an old car roughly five blocks from the highway. The two guys jumped up and grabbed their AK-47s out of the car's trunk and fired in the highway's direction a couple of runs each, and that started a chain reaction.

Gunfire exploded throughout the neighborhood. The 9mm, the M16s, the .45s, the homemade shotguns, and the coveted AK47s.' The staccatos of the guns scared the decent people of the neighborhood.

Shooting stars landed all over the barrio. The bullets' cracks and whistles flew in all directions.

The crescendo of the heavy shooting arrived at the police station like a shock wave. Vitalino Tahuite got out of his office and went to the main entrance of the station. There he found six policemen lying on the floor with guns drawn.

"I was hoping you could go out there and apprehend those people," he said jokingly. The six officers on the floor laughed at his badly spoken Spanish. Vitalino thought they were laughing at his joke, and they all laughed out loud.

A police car came to a screeching halt outside the station. Two policemen jumped out and ran to the entrance, bullets buzzing too close to their ears as if those bullets were disrespectful mosquitos.

As soon as the two policemen entered the station and locked the double metal door, Vitalino Tahuite called his men to his office, the only room protected with a double brick wall. There they sat down to drink coffee and wait for the Angel of Death to fly over their heads.

The gunfire lasted over forty minutes, all because, in the barrio, bullets are cheaper than food, medicine, and gasoline. Only when the heroic firemen's blaring sirens ran through the width and length of the neighborhood looking for the dead and the wounded, did the police besiege the barrio.

The little or no willingness of the police to enforce law and order, and their constant comedy of bullying the decent residents and letting the criminals go free, enraged the respectable residents of the neighborhood.

The neighbors of the barrio's economic situation did not allow them to live elsewhere. The residents hurled insults of the lowest kind to the police, but the respectable residents were always easy prey, and as is always the case, they were arrested.

It was early morning when the shootout ended. Mariano got up from behind the hillock by the highway's edge, where he had enjoyed the forty minutes that the gunfire lasted. He phoned a tow truck to take his vehicle to a body shop and waited for the tow truck.

While waiting for the tow truck to arrive, Mariano took the stones and broken glass out of his pickup. When the last stone was out of his car, he walked around his vehicle trying to estimate the cost to repair the damage.

On his vehicle's left side, he found another message written in big capital letters and between parentheses: "CHE LIVES." Che Guevara was a Latin American revolutionary. In response, Mariano took a piece of broken glass and wrote in big capital letters under that message, "IN HELL WWW.HELL.COM." When he finished writing his statement, he smiled.

Mariano was looking at the damage done to his pickup's interior with his back to the highway. Suddenly, he felt surrounded. He turned around and was surprised to see his friends; he kneeled and embraced them all with his arms wide open.

"Where have you been?" he asked, not expecting an answer. The dogs licked his face and wagged their tails, happy to see him. Mariano opened the doors of his double cabin pickup truck and invited them in, but to his amazement, the dogs hugged and kissed each other to say goodbye in their own way.

Cinderella, Cindy, Anaximenes, and Anaximander got in the car, while Peregrino, Bella, Lucky, and Fortunato, standing on their hind legs, hugged Mariano and licked his hands and face. That done, they turned around and left. At that moment, Mariano fell into a strange trance and was unable to move; he just stood there, unaware of the world around him.

When he came out of that strange state, he tried to run after his friends, but the tow truck got in his way.

"You call a tow truck?" said the driver, a burly man with a salt and pepper beard and rough manners.

Mariano had come out of the strange trance with a splitting headache and was not in the mood to take a bad attitude from anyone. Not turning his head to see the tow truck driver, he muttered, "Yeah."

Mariano gave the tow truck driver the address of the place they were going. The tow truck driver did what he needed to do, and they were gone.

ASSYRIA, BABYLON AND GENGHIS KHAN

Eight weeks had passed following their siblings' decision to go with Mariano and rendezvous with their destiny. A couple of hours before dawn, Lucky woke up startled from a nightmare. In his nightmare he saw himself standing on a rock, watching Peregrino walk across a newly paved road toward him. Suddenly, the road turned into a raging black ink river. Peregrino tried swimming to the rock where Lucky was standing but could not make it, and the strong current dragged him along with it.

Lucky, fearing for his brother's life, jumped into the water to try to save him, but the moment he hit the raging river, he sank in it like a bronze sculpture. On his way to the bottom of that river, his eyes turned the color of the ink that surrounded him, and he knew then that he was lost.

Startled and shaking, Lucky opened his mouth wide and greedily breathed loads of air. When he opened his eyes, he could not see anything. Everything was dark, and for a moment, Lucky felt as if he still was in his most recent nightmare. Fortunately for him, Bella's snoring brought him back to reality. Lucky immediately pawed around in the dark, trying to find Peregrino, as he always did whenever he woke from a bad dream or a nightmare. When he could not find his brother, he woke Bella and Fortunato up, and the three of them went out of the cave looking for Peregrino.

Once outside the cave, they picked up Peregrino's unmistakable scent drifting in the air and inviting them to follow it. They did follow it, and it guided them in the direction of the highway. When they reached the hillock by the road's edge, they saw a lonely silhouette sitting there. "Peregrino!" exclaimed Fortunato, and the three of them ran toward him.

"It's about time you showed up," said Peregrino when they came to his side.

"How did you know we were coming?" asked Lucky.

"A little bird told me," answered Peregrino.

"Are we going somewhere?" asked Bella, but somehow, she knew the answer to her question. "Duck hunting?" she asked.

"Duck hunting," said Peregrino, nodding affirmatively. Then he added, "That is, if you are willing and able.

"We are! We are!" said Fortunato, wagging his tail excitedly.

"We are more than willing and able," said Lucky, a little concerned about his brother's health. "But you are not out of the woods yet." As an answer to Lucky's worries, Peregrino stood on his hind legs and walked around a little; the shaking was gone, and so was Beethoven's 5th Symphony.

"Now, please pay attention and do as I do." That said, Peregrino looked to the right and the left of the highway. Dawn was not yet born, so the road was quiet. When he was sure there was no danger, he ran across to the median that divided the highway and waited there for the others to get across.

Bella, Fortunato, and Lucky, emulating Peregrino's road crossing skills, looked to the left and right. When they were about to run across and join Peregrino at the median, they came face to face with Guapo, the handsome devil of the highway.

"Good morning, brave travelers!" said Guapo graciously, while bending his left front leg, bowing his head, and touching his chest, lips, and forehead with his right paw, greeting them Arab style.

"Don't listen to him. Don't even look at him," Peregrino yelled at them from the median. But it was too late; the three of them were already under the spell of Guapo of the highway. But how could they not be? How could they resist his magic? Was he not so charming? Was he not so beautiful that it was impossible not to look at him, not to listen to him?

"My lady, would you allow this humble knight to help you across this dangerous path?" said Guapo in a breathtaking, exotic, and exquisite accent which could melt any female dog's heart.

Bella, feeling like a princess in a fairy tale, closed her eyes and gently touched Guapo's extended paw. Guapo held Bella close to his chest and standing on their hind legs, slowly crossed toward the median while dancing Johann Strauss' "Blue Danube," followed by Lucky and Fortunato. Out of the shadows and the mist of the unborn dawn, came the lights of a sports car traveling at extreme speed. Lucky and Fortunato felt their bodies heavier than lead, and in a state in which they could not discern between reality and a dream, saw everything moving before their eyes in slow motion.

Before Bella and Guapo could take another step, Peregrino, his fangs bared, pounced on Guapo with all his might. But he could not touch him, as Guapo had vanished in thin air, and Bella bore the brunt of the attack. Bella and Peregrino went rolling back to the edge of the road. Peregrino's action broke the spell. Lucky and Fortunato instinctively jumped back to the road's edge, but the car had already passed, brushing the tips of their noses. As soon as Lucky, Bella, and Fortunato were back to their usual selves, they shook their heads vigorously to eliminate the last bit of brain-numbing spell.

"Okay, it was my fault," said Peregrino, a little angry with himself for failing to warn his family of the danger called Guapo. "We will do it together this time. Look to your right, look to your left, and let us go."

When they reached the other side of the highway, Peregrino said to his family, "We made it, but always be wary when crossing this path. Always do it before dawn and never look at or listen to Guapo."

When they looked up the trail they had to follow, they saw Guapo standing on a big rock by the side of the road. "Close your eyes and let me be your guide," said Peregrino.

"Get in line behind me, and whatever you do, do not turn your head to see Guapo unless you want to turn into stone," warned Peregrino.

"Stone!" exclaimed Fortunato.

"Yes, that evil spirit has the power to do that, so heed my words."

They closed their eyes and as they walked past the big rock where Guapo was standing, Bella fell into the temptation to see the beautiful dog one more time. She instantly stopped breathing and moving, and just stood there in the middle of the trail as if she was a stone sculpture.

"Peregrino the enlightened one! Lucky the dog killer! Fortunato the dauntless! And Bella the beautiful," said Guapo amicably. Then he added, "Good hunting! Good friends! Great adventures! Farewell, farewell. I know our paths will cross again, Peregrino, but today you shall leave a part of you with me."

Those words, shrouded in mystery and a possible threat, made the boys stop in their tracks. They opened their eyes and turned to see Guapo, only to realize that Bella was not with them. She was standing in the middle of the trail, like a lifeless marble replica of herself. When Lucky turned into a terrifying fury of teeth and claws and was about to run and pounce on Guapo, Peregrino, making a tremendous effort, managed to calm him down, but not before getting nasty bites on his neck and shoulders. Once calmed down, Lucky looked for an answer to what was happening in his brother's eyes, but what he saw in those eyes made him sit and be still.

Peregrino took an instant to control his anger and to turn himself into an amiable dog. That accomplished, he turned around and, wagging his tail in a friendly way, approached Guapo. And as if talking to himself aloud, said: "where did I meet him the first time? Was it in Babylon? Assyria? Or the Persian empire?"

Guapo, wagging his tail, excitedly decided to play Peregrino's game. As if talking to himself, he said aloud, "Wasn't he Cleopatra's backside licking little lapdog?"

Peregrino, looking at Guapo straight in his eyes and making a tremendous effort not to laugh, said, "Weren't you Genghis Khan's first love and then his supper? Because those Asians eat dogs, don't they?" They looked at each other's eyes and then threw themselves to the ground and laughed out loud in the way only dogs know how to do.

When they stopped laughing, Guapo said, "He sure was a crazy guy, wasn't he?" And they laughed a little more. Peregrino, seeing Guapo in such a good mood, saw his chance to save Bella, so he said to him while pointing at Bella with his nose, "Can you give her back to us?"

"Why not? After all, it wouldn't be the first time I gave her back to you." Peregrino tried not to look surprised, but Guapo saw the surprise in his eyes and said, "If you don't believe me, ask Fortunato. He was there."

Earnestly looking at Peregrino, Guapo said to him, "I will be happy to give her back to you, only this time I want something in return. What have you to barter?"

"What does a dog possess?" said Peregrino. "A dog could find monies, sometimes jewelry, and sometimes even gold. But a dog has not a saddle bag to carry it, a dog only has his life to offer. And when he lays down his life for a loved one, he gives his life as one who offers a rose, as one who gives a kiss, and a dog does not have to think twice about it."

"Are you telling me you are willing to give your life for her?"

"I am, but not this day, not now."

"Yeah, not today, not now," said Guapo, a bit disappointed.

"Not now, not ever," shouted Lucky, his back hair standing on end as he showed his fangs. Guapo looked at Lucky, and again he saw something in Lucky he could not decipher.

Guapo approached Bella and whispered in one of her ears, "Wake up, Bella." Bella woke up, and as she opened her eyes and found herself face to face with Guapo, she was overwhelmed with a mixture of happiness and sadness.

"I know you, right?" said Bella. Guapo nodded, and she saw a faint smile in his eyes. "Yes, I am sure I know you from somewhere." She walked away to join Lucky and Fortunato, but halfway there, she turned around and ran to the spot where Guapo was standing.

Bella's memories were like an incomplete jigsaw puzzle. Images of an island paradise of a previous life came to her, but that was enough to remember a little bit of that prior life.

"Now I remember you. You never said goodbye, what happened to you? I fell into a deep and dark hole in the ground hidden among some bushes where I was trying to catch a rabbit. My ancient bones are still there. My ancient bones got old waiting for you," said Bella. Then, she turned around and went to join her family.

"Lucky," said Guapo aloud before disappearing, "if you expect to live to a ripe old age, learn to control your anger; do not unleash your fury all at once. Save some for the next day." That said, he was gone.

Peregrino and his family stood there watching the big ornamental rock where Guapo had been standing. "How come he knows our names and where we're going?" asked Fortunato.

"I was about to ask the same question," said Lucky.

Peregrino explained to them briefly who that extraordinary dog was.

"The herald of death!" exclaimed Fortunato. At the same time, his back hair, as well as Lucky's and Bella's hair, stood on end as well. And a shudder coursed through their bodies back and forth.

"Not Death's herald, but one of her assistants," said Peregrino. "The difference between this one and the others, is that this one has powers that can lead you to your death. Unlike the others that kindly and tenderly help you across to the other side, this one is evil and enjoys the violent deaths of his brothers and sisters. The more violent the demise, the more enjoyable for him. The more dogs die under his evil influence, the closer he gets to his objective, which is to become death itself and take the world as his territory." That said, Peregrino finished by saying, "Guapo has the power to go anywhere his heart desires, but he has chosen this highway as his territory because of the many dogs that violently die here."

"Does he mark it?" asked Fortunato.

"He does when a dog dies on his turf, I smelled it the day he led Mona to her death."

Peregrino fell silent and stood with downcast eyes for a few seconds, and then he said, "I feel bad every time I remember Mona. She was so beautiful and young and pure. I blame myself for her death because I did nothing to protect her." That said, he lowered his head and fell silent again, staring sadly at the ground.

"When Mona died, you were also too young and too innocent. You didn't know what you know now," said Bella, trying to cheer him up.

Peregrino nodded and said, "I left Mona's lifeless body on that big rock where Guapo was standing." They all looked at the big rock with sad eyes, and for an instant that only lasted as long as a dog's heartbeat, they thought they saw Mona looking at them and wagging her tail.

"For reasons unknown to me," said Peregrino, breaking the silence they had fallen in. "that evil being does not influence me. I can see him as he really is. Believe you me, he is not as beautiful as he appears at all, but on the contrary, you need a tremendous intestinal fortitude not to vomit or run away shaking in terror."

Bella, Lucky, and Fortunato had no words to express the overwhelming feelings of pride and happiness that were overflowing in their hearts, to know themselves to be an essential part of Peregrino's life, so they silently went to kiss him.

MEMENTO MORI

The immeasurable red-hot ball in the sky was vaporizing the last few dew pearls in Ares and Nikus' ravine. The beauty of those dew pearls did not diminish, whether they rested on the most beautiful and exotic flowers in the world or on the wildflowers growing intertwined with the garbage in Ares and Nikus' ravine. Peregrino and his clan searched for Ares and Nikus high and low, following the smell of their urine with which they had marked their territory, but they could not find them. Lucky suggested they go to the hollow in the old tree trunk, their friend's lair. There they picked up Nikus' scent, which was in the air mixed with a faint patchouli scent. Following that mixture of smells, they found themselves at María Margarita's doorstep. María Margarita's front door was ajar as always. Peregrino pushed it hard to make sure the little bells hanging behind the door would sound, and immediately four big dogs went to welcome them. The four dogs sniffed them thoroughly and then led them to the living room through a wide and long hallway. At the end of that hallway was the living room, and lying on the floor were six dogs.

Two of the dogs lying on the floor recognized Lucky and immediately jumped to their feet, bared their teeth, snarled, and went to block their way. One of the dogs blocking the newcomer's way had a horrible scar on his face's left side, and his left eye kept staring at the ground. When the other four dogs in the living room heard the racket in the hallway, they jumped up and went to stand by the side of Dropped Eye, as the dog with the scar was known.

"These murderers are not welcome here," shouted a dog whose name was Chalo. Then he added, "These two are the ones that killed Belshazzar." That said, he began chanting, "Persians, Persians, Persians, damn you Persians, murderers, murderers, murderers. Mene, Mene Tekel Upharsin, Mene, Mene Tekel Upharsin." When the other four dogs joined in the chant, they turned into a canine choir.

As soon as Peregrino and company growled and bared their teeth, ready to defend themselves, one of the dogs in charge of welcoming the newcomers nipped the problem in the bud before it became a fight.

The dog said aloud to the choir boys with a razor-sharp tone of voice, "I sincerely hope you boys are thinking about breaking the number one rule of this sacred place, because if you are, that would be just wonderful."

"I enjoy the little party that comes after someone breaks the number one rule," he said sarcastically. And his sharp words slashed the spirits of the six dogs, who hastily moved out of the way.

As the dog who had reminded Dropped Eye and his buddies of the punishment for breaking the number one rule walked past the troublemakers, he said sardonically, "Too bad you boys changed your mind. We have not had one of those dainty parties in a long time."

As soon as Dropped Eye and his buddies remembered the punishment for breaking the Halfway to Heaven Hotel's number one rule, they stuck to the hallway wall with their tails tucked between their legs and their heads dropped and looking at the floor.

The number one rule was unknown to María Margarita, but well known to every dog of the barrio. The number one rule stipulated that no dog shall fight, no dog shall join others to fight inside, outside, or near the Halfway to Heaven Hotel, out of respect and love for María Margarita. The punishment for breaking the number one rule was known as the African dance of death. The dogs executed the African dance on the barrio's west side, far away from María Margarita's home.

The punishment consisted of standing the offender in the center of a circle made up of the barrio's dogs, where all the dogs bit the offender mercilessly. The violent attack forced the offender to perform a frantic and mortal dance.

The offender, trying to avoid some of the attackers' teeth, places his flesh in the other dogs' teeth. When the offender is exhausted, out of his mind, and in terrible pain, he falls to the ground. Very few dogs ever survived the African dance of death. Consequently, no dog in his right mind was willing to break the number one rule.

During the African dance of death, the number of injured or dead dogs increases because some inner circle dogs get accidentally pushed to the circle's center. There, they are mauled not only by the offender but also by the executioners, since a frenzy of rage seizes all the participants.

"We will be waiting for you outside," said one of Dropped Eye's buddies as Peregrino walked near him, but Peregrino ignored him.

Hate and fury were boiling in Dropped Eye's innards. He had his brother's killers so close yet so unreachable because of the number one rule, which had stopped him from killing them now that they were six against three and a youngster. The number one rule denied Dropped Eye his sweet revenge, and that had his innards boiling, including his heart and throat. That compelled him to say to Peregrino as he passed by his side, "We found you guilty of murder, and you must pay for your sins." Peregrino ignored him as he had ignored the words of one of his buddies. Lucky, who was walking behind his brother, glowered at the six dogs and said to them in a dead language, "Memento Mori!" Those words, which were a reminder of death, made Chalo drop to the floor as he remembered that Lucky had sent him on a short visit to Xibalba, the Mayan underworld.

When Dropped Eye saw Chalo's attitude, he gritted his teeth in anger, and in an angry tone of voice, said to his buddies as he headed to the exit, "Let us go, boys. I know lots of guys who would love to get in a fight." His friends followed him, with Chalo gloomily bringing up the rear.

DIGGING A GRAVE

The dog that had reminded Dropped Eye and his buddies of the number one rule left Peregrino and company in the living room, saying they should wait there for María Margarita. "She is having a siesta," he said as he headed for the back yard with the other three dogs.

"Peregrino! What a pleasant surprise!" exclaimed María Margarita when she came to the living room. And when she had kissed and hugged Peregrino and his family, she talked to them a long while as if they could understand what she was saying.

Peregrino and family did not speak María Margarita's language, but her soft and sweet voice was music that filled their hearts with joy as much as if they understood every word that came out of her mouth.

Some eight dogs napping around the living room woke up as soon as they heard María Margarita's sweet voice and immediately greeted her happily and excitedly, wagging their tails as if they had not seen her in ages.

María Margarita led Peregrino and his family to the back yard. The dogs lying here and there got up and went to greet her with hugs and kisses and immediately joined the walk to the back yard in an orderly fashion, despite their selfish desire to be the only ones to get her love and caresses.

María Margarita always took her sweet time with every dog, hugging and kissing them and calling them by name, which she knew by heart since she named every dog that came in her house.

As they approached the back yard through a long corridor, they came to a bedroom, the door of which was ajar. The unfurnished bedroom María Margarita had given to Lady.

Lady was an unfriendly, big and robust female Rottweiler dog. María Margarita opened the door wide and entered Lady's bedroom to check on her and her newborn babies. Lady was feeding her babies. When she saw María Margarita, she tried to get up, but María Margarita signaled her to stay.

María Margarita caressed Lady and her four babies. When she was satisfied that Lady and her babies were fine, and that Lady had enough food and water, María Margarita went out of the room.

None of the dogs walking with her to the back yard had dared to go into Lady's bedroom, because they all knew that Lady would shred to pieces any dog stupid enough to come close to her babies.

"Peregrino," said María Margarita with a big smile. "I have a surprise for you. Two of your friends are here among us. Nikus loves children, so I guess some of those children used a whole bottle of perfume on him. Can you smell the sweet scent? I am sure you do; after all, you are a dog."

Peregrino did not understand a single word that came out of María Margarita's mouth, though listening to her sweet voice was good enough for him.

Some ten dogs were sleeping in various spots throughout the back yard. A cute little dachshund named Memo, the only constant resident in the Halfway to Heaven Hotel, was the first to spot María Margarita coming into the back yard. Memo immediately barked loudly, saying to the other dogs, "María is here, María is here." All the dogs woke up, and when they saw their goddess, they immediately got up and went to greet her.

With so many dogs in a house, it is easy to imagine all the kaka all over the place. But not in the Halfway to Heaven Hotel. One of the unbreakable rules of the site stipulated that no dog shall poop, wee, or mark territory inside, outside, or near the Halfway to Heaven Hotel. They all did it in the garbage dump, unless they were too sick to walk. Every dog followed this rule out of love and respect for their goddess.

Because of the great multitude of dogs milling around María Margarita, Ares and Nikus couldn't see their friends. María Margarita knew it, so she grabbed Nikus by the neck and pushed him toward Peregrino.

"Peregrino!" exclaimed Nikus aloud.

"Peregrino? How? When? And where?" asked Ares out loud while trying to find his friend in that sea of fanning tails. He wiggled himself through the crowd until he came face to face with Lucky.

Ares pounced on Lucky, and the two friends went rolling on the floor, immensely happy to see each other. Before they could get up from the floor, Nikus jumped on Lucky, and Peregrino jumped on Ares, and inadvertently, the four friends rolled to the center of a circle formed by the rest of the dogs in the back yard. Not caring what the reason for those boys' happiness was, all the dogs there felt as happy as those four.

María Margarita shared the overflowing and genuine happiness of the dogs. She and all the dogs felt like a deluge of joy was falling on them.

María Margarita entered the circle with a radiant smile. As she bent down to caress the four friends, she said to them in a soft and sweet voice, "I am sure you boys have a lot to talk about and a lot of stories to tell each other, but I have a job to do and I must do it right now. She called Bella and Fortunato to the center of the circle of dogs. Peregrino, Ares, and Nikus left Lucky inside the circle and went out of it.

María Margarita took in her hands Bella's, Fortunato's, and Lucky's heads and said solemnly, "Let us be silent to be able to hear the voice of the wind." Except for Bella, Lucky, and Fortunato, all the dogs knew the name-giving ritual, so they closed their eyes and were silent.

María Margarita raised her arms and eyes to heaven and performed a short Moorish dance. That done, she invoked the wind's spirit with the mystical words passed on to her from her maternal grandmother as her only legacy.

"Caudapede, Caudapede, Caniscauda. Alviniaventus, Alviniaventus. Maure, maure, maure. Shehabcanis, Shehabcanis. vini, vini, vini ventus vini."

The wind's spirit response was not long in coming. María Margarita heard the wind whisper in her ears as soft and as gentle as the almost imperceptible fluttering of a hummingbird.

"Lucky, Fortunato, Belladona. Lucky, Fortunato, Belladona," María Margarita repeated. "Lucky, Fortunato, Belladona." All the dogs in the back yard repeated the same words in their own way.

All the dogs in the back yard welcomed the newcomers to the family once the name-giving ritual was over. Suddenly, out of nowhere, a cold wave hit the gathering. The cold wave was ice needles puncturing their flesh and bones.

The dogs shook their bodies vigorously, trying to shake away the cold and the chills that were coursing back and forth through their bodies, like a ravenous flea swarm that was biting their flesh. But no matter how much they tried, they could not shake it off.

Utterly bewildered, his mouth wide open and trapped in an electrifying trance from which he unsuccessfully was trying to break free, Peregrino heard himself say out loud, "The herald of demise walks among us." Peregrino's words were like pails of extremely cold-water cascading on all those in the back yard and that made their hair stand on end, and while some dogs were weeping and gnashing their teeth, other dogs' teeth were flamenco dancer's castanets chattering loudly, including María Margarita's teeth.

María Margarita hugged herself tightly, trying to ease the shuddering that was shaking her violently. That reminded her she had left her favorite cardigan on one of the dining room chairs, so she decided to go in and get it. When she was walking by Lady's bedroom, she went in to make sure everything was all right with her and her babies. The blood-curdling sight María Margarita encountered in the middle of that room made her scream in terror. Her piercing scream reverberated all over the house. She screamed when she saw Guapo in his creepiest appearance standing next to Lady, who under his evil influence was devouring her babies. It was too much for María Margarita; she covered her eyes with her hands and fell to the floor.

When all the dogs in the house came to their goddess' aid, they saw Lady's fangs dripping blood and saliva and ready to attack the only human who had shown her love and kindness. Standing next to her was Guapo in his most putrid appearance. Dry skin strips were hanging from his fleshless face. His lifeless eyes were out of their cavities and a bunch of maggots were feeding on his scattered guts on the floor. That frightening sight turned the dogs into savage beasts, and they pounced simultaneously on Guapo and Lady as well.

When María Margarita came to, she was apprehensive about opening her eyes, so she opened them slowly. When she saw the heartbreaking sight she had in front of her, she did everything humanly possible to lose consciousness again, but all her efforts were in vain. She had no choice but to face the gruesome reality. There was Lady dead in a puddle of blood, her fangs stuck in little Memo's throat.

María Margarita sat on the cold floor crying for what seemed to her a long time. When she couldn't shed any more tears, she tried to get up, but her body was numbed with cold from the waist down. María Margarita couldn't get up, so she dragged herself along the floor to the dining room, and when she reached the dining table, making a tremendous effort, she managed to stand up with the help of two of the chairs.

María Margarita threw on her favorite cardigan and began strolling back and forth from the dining room to the living room. When the numbness and the pain diminished, she headed to the back yard to dig a grave.

María Margarita was not a young woman, so thirty minutes of digging with a pick and a shovel left her exhausted and thirsty. She stopped digging and went to the kitchen for a glass of water and a little break. And that gave the professionals the opportunity they were waiting for. All the dogs got in the hole, and by the time it took María Margarita to return to the hole, the grave was ready to be used.

When María Margarita finished burying Memo, Lady, and her babies, she gazed up to heaven and lifted her arms to say a little prayer for her dead friends. Exhausted and with deep sorrow in her heart, she went to bed. Peregrino, his family and friends, decided to stay in the Halfway to Heaven Hotel to help her deal with her grief. With the passing of the days and thanks to the everyday love and caresses from the dogs, María Margarita gradually regained her well-being. Little by little, the sadness in her heart and on her countenance faded away.

Twenty days passed after the burials of Memo, Lady, and her babies. At this time, Peregrino, his family, and his friends, happy and satisfied to see the goddess of the Halfway to Heaven Hotel back to her sweet and smiling old self, went to say their goodbyes. By then, most of the dogs had left the place.

María Margarita, with abundant tears in her eyes, thanked them for their kind gesture and noble hearts. She then placed Peregrino's face in both her hands and said,

"I know you are not like any other dog; you are one in many thousands.

There is something ineffable, something so esoteric in you that I can't decipher. I also know that a great adventure awaits all of you, but you must be wary for there is something evil constantly following you. For some strange reason it can't harm you, but it can bring danger, suffering, and death to those close to your heart, and that includes me."

Peregrino, utterly bewildered, couldn't discern whether he was daydreaming or if it was his imagination when he understood every word that came out of María Margarita's mouth. And that corroborated the wisdom in Nikus' reasoning when he said that she was an enlightened one, that day when he met her the first time, which to Peregrino seemed like a lifetime ago. Not knowing what to say or do, he stood on his hind legs and kissed her.

The dogs kissed their goddess goodbye. When she finished kissing all of them, she reminded them that her house was also their house. "You know you can come here any day, any time. The door, like my heart and my arms, will always be open for you, and if someday you find yourselves sick or badly injured, come to me even if you must crawl on the ground to get here. I will heal your wounds, and if you arc too sick or if your injuries are too severe that I can't heal them, rest assured that with lots of love and without pain, I will open the gates of heaven for you. Please, whatever you do, don't let me find you dead by the side of a road."

None of the dogs understood what María Margarita was saying this time, but they knew she loved them, and that was more than enough for them. Wagging their tails, they stood on their hind legs and kissed her one more time, then they turned around and headed for the door.

María Margarita followed the dogs to the door where she leaned on the doorframe to steady herself as she watched her friends go. "Fare thee well, my children," she said out loud, and the dogs turned around to give her one last look. From the first moment he saw her, Fortunato became captive of the pure love she radiated. He couldn't help himself, so he ran back to give her one last kiss. As she hugged him, he felt there was something of Uncle Pirate's love in her heart.

ALI BABA

---◆◆◆---

O nly two dogs decided to stay at the Halfway to Heaven Hotel. One of those two dogs walked with the boys for a short distance. To see him walking by their side aroused Ares and Nikus' curiosity. They didn't know that dog, even though they knew all the dogs in the neighborhood and beyond. Nikus, trying to find out why that dog was walking with them, approached him and said, "I know you, right?"

"Nope," said the dog while looking back at the Halfway to Heaven Hotel, and not even looking at Nikus added, "but I know who you are."

Nikus' curiosity hit the ceiling. Visibly excited, he asked the dog, "How do you know who I am?"

The dog paused for a second before answering, and then he whispered as if he was afraid to be heard. "A hot afternoon in a faraway place," said the dog. The minute the dog said it, the friends looked at him astounded, because the dog's words came out slurred and sprayed with loads of saliva from one side of his mouth.

The dog continued with his story, undaunted by the looks of astonishment on the faces of his listeners. "I came to a house that was casting a lovely cool shade and lay down at the door. I hadn't been lying there very long when a little human boy opened the door and offered me water. When the little boy felt that I wouldn't harm him, he let me in the house and fed me all kinds of Italian food. While I gorged myself with Italian food, he showed me many images of yourself with something written on them. I guess I will never know what that writing said."

He went on, "Before opening the door to let me out, the little boy, crying his eyes out, said many things to me while pointing at your image with his little fingers. All I could understand was that your name is Copernicus. I guessed he was telling me to tell you to go home to him."

"Angelo! Angelo! Mio Angelo," cried Nikus as he threw himself to the ground, where between sobs he repeatedly professed his great fault in Latin, "Mea culpa! Mea culpa! Mea maxima culpa!"

"A few days later," the dog continued saying and spraying everyone with saliva, "as I was trying to get to the famous Halfway to Heaven Hotel, some dogs I met informed me that I had to cross the scary highway called Death's Path and face the handsome, evil dog they call Guapo to get here."

He continued, "To avoid falling under the evil influence of Guapo, I closed my eyes and ran across the highway. Fortunately, I was hit and not run over by one of the speeding cars traveling there. I jumped up when I stopped cartwheeling and sliding, and I went running with my eyes closed again. When I thought I was safe, I opened my eyes and found myself on the spot where I had started running. And who was there waiting for me? None other than Guapo, who was laughing his guts out."

The dog went on, "Under the influence of Guapo, I couldn't move. When he stopped laughing, he said to me, 'because you made me laugh and believe me, no one makes me laugh, I will help you get to the other side.' I said, 'no thanks, when my time comes, I will need no help to cross over to the other side.' and he said, 'Not that side, you dumb dumb. I mean the other side of the highway. But you will have to deliver a message to someone I know.' I asked him what kind of message, and he said that he would have to tell me when we got to the other side of the highway.

"When we reached the other side of the highway, I was so frightened, that I had to run to the nearest tree to pee. When I got to the tree, Guapo was already there waiting for me. 'I want you to tell Nikus that I am waiting for him,'" he said. "I asked who Nikus is, and as an answer, he pointed at an image of you stuck on the tree and then he vanished. That image on the tree was undoubtedly the same as the ones little Angelo showed me at his home."

After a short pause, the dog said to Nikus, "Whenever you want to see your Angelo, come to see me at the Halfway to Heaven Hotel, and I will take you to him." Nikus was still lying on the floor, feeling guilty, and didn't thank the dog for all the information he had provided.

The dog looked back at María Margarita's house, and when he felt sure that she wouldn't be able to hear him, he said to Peregrino aloud, "I know that Dropped Eye has an ambush set up for you guys, so beware."

Ares, a tad annoyed, said to the dog, "Can you give us a little more information about this ambush you are talking about?"

"All I know is that Dropped Eye is planning to do a lot of harm to your friends." That said, the dog turned around and said, "I got to go back; I don't want troubles with Dropped Eye, so please don't mention my name and remember, what you just heard did not come out of my mouth."

Ares and friends looked at each other and they made a tremendous effort not to laugh, because the words did not seem to come out of his mouth but from his right cheek.

Ares promised they would never mention his name, not only because they were grateful for all the information about Nikus' little brother Angelo and the warning about Dropped Eye's ambush, but mainly because they did not know his name.

"My name is Ali. I am not from this land. I'm sure you know Guatemalan dogs are famous for giving other dogs nicknames, so I am mostly known as Ali Baba. Baba means drool in Spanish, the dog said, as if he didn't know the dogs he was talking to were Guatemalans.

As he finished talking, he wiped with his tongue the stream of drool off his right cheek and lower right lip, which was hanging loosely and to one side of his face, which gave him the appearance of suffering from some facial paralysis.

"I see," said Ares, and thanked him again. Ali nodded and headed back to María Margarita's house. When he was about to go into the house, Nikus jumped up from the floor and shouted at Ali, "Thank you for the information, Ali. I will look for you when I am ready to see Angelo."

Ali wagged his tail as an answer and disappeared behind the door.

Ares and Nikus didn't know the reason for their friends and Dropped Eye's enmity toward each other, so they asked Peregrino for an explanation. Peregrino, not wanting to give the matter much importance, said, "Lucky and I had a friendly encounter with Dropped Eye, his brother Belshazzar, and their sidekick Chalo when they were trying to take over our territory.

"That day, our mild-mannered brother Lucky, who wouldn't hurt a fly, sent Belshazzar to meet his maker, and he also sent Chalo on a short tour of the realm of the dead as well."

Bella, Fortunato, Ares, and Nikus looked at Lucky with great admiration and simultaneously pounced on him, hugging and kissing him. Peregrino, satisfied with his recognition of his brother's bravery, stood there watching his family and friends with a broad smile in his eyes.

"Now I will tell you the rest of the story," said Lucky, visibly excited. "Let everyone know that it was Peregrino who bestowed all the beauty upon Dropped Eye's face." Family and friends looked at Peregrino admiringly, and then they all pounced on him, and the hugging and kissing continued.

When their little celebration ended, Ares said to Lucky, "Now tell us the whole story, brother Lucky."

Lucky did not have to be asked twice about telling a story, so he told the story with a wealth of details and ended it by saying, "Thanks to the intervention of one of the dogs in charge of welcoming the visits that day at the Halfway to Heaven Hotel, all hell did not break loose."

As soon as Lucky finished telling the story, Nikus said, "I know that you guys are not the kind of dogs that lose sleep thinking about dogs like the good for nothing Dropped Eye, but let me tell you a little about him just for laughs. For me, Dropped Eye is like an unloved and physically abused child."

"How so?" asked Fortunato.

"I rarely see him, but I always beat the stuffing out of him when I do. I hope with all my heart to see him today. I miss him," said Nikus while feigning a sad sigh.

The smiles in his friends' eyes encouraged Nikus to keep talking. "Ah yes, he said, I almost forgot to mention that our friend Ares here is known as the mean father of all the dogs in the neighborhood and beyond. Can you guys guess why?"

The friends continued talking, joking, and walking until they came to the end of the street, which flowed like a river into the naked avenue. The nude lane was a broad and long dirt road covered with a layer of white sand. That road separated the endless row of houses from the ravine.

Dropped Eye, and some fifteen of his cronies were at the dirt road called the naked avenue waiting for Peregrino and his family, and they all were ready to do a lot of harm.

Lucky's eyes were ice as he stared at Chalo while walking directly toward him. And that reminded Chalo of his short visit to the underworld, and he bolted out of the battlefield.

Dropped Eye saw Nikus coming directly at him with bared fangs, and he decided that it was not a good idea to wait for him, so he took off from the fighting ground.

The rest of the ambushers lost their resolve when they saw big Ares coming at them with bad intentions, and they too, withdrew from the battlefield in a hurry.

Only one dog stood his ground, standing firmly on his four feet, his fangs ready and growling as he waited for Ares. All the dogs retreating from the battlefield turned around and asked themselves, "Is that an extraordinarily brave dog or an extraordinarily stupid dog?"

When Ares was about to give that dog the most painful lesson of his life, Peregrino stopped him, and they watched Fortunato jump on the dog and grab him by one of his ears and shake him violently.

When Lucky tried to stop Bella, it was too late. Bella was a bolt of lightning falling on the poor dog. The dog went rolling on the ground, and before he could get up, Bella sank her canines into the dog's backside.

The dog managed to escape from Bella's teeth and ran away crying with his tail between his legs. That dog became known by the dogs of the barrio as stupid for the rest of his life.

Fortunato was standing there with a smile in his eyes, watching Stupid the dog run away. Nikus, standing on his hind legs, hugged Fortunato and said, "Well done, my boy. If you continue fighting like you did today, one day you will be as good a fighter as your Uncle Nikus."

"I hope so, Uncle Nikus. I hope so," said young Fortunato.

KOBE AND THE ALBINO

W hen the last one of the ambushers was gone, Peregrino and his entourage stood in the middle of the naked avenue. They looked at the horizon and thought about the adventures that awaited them. All of them excitedly took the first step toward their next adventure and to their destiny.

The ravine's edge and its slopes were full of flowering blue jacaranda trees, and flowering bougainvillea shrubs shaped like small trees embellished the whitewashed houses' front lawn.

Far in the distance, where the white sand naked avenue suddenly veered left and disappeared, to the beholder's eye, the jacaranda tree's light blue flowers appeared as if intertwined with the pink, red, orange, yellow, and magenta of the bougainvillea flowers, in an imaginary sandy white vase. And behind that fanciful vase of overflowing, colorful flowers which the distance turned into butterflies, the mountain range stood as if floating in the horizon's mist.

Peregrino and his traveling companions put Dropped Eye and his cronies out of their heads and joyfully began their march toward the duck pond. They were not in a hurry to get there, so they adopted a carefree step.

As the friends moved along, they enjoyed the scenery. Like ancient mariners tempted by the alluring songs of mythological sirens, they too were enticed by the exotic smells of the foods cooked, in the kitchens of the row of houses to the left of the naked avenue.

They had not been walking not even for twenty minutes, when suddenly and for no apparent reason, Peregrino, the leader in that expedition and who was walking a few steps ahead of the group, stopped his joyful march. He stood there as if hypnotized. It happened so fast that he did not have time to finish his step. One of his front legs and one of his rear legs remained up in the air.

When Peregrino's traveling companions saw him so still as if he was a petrified dog, they looked at the road ahead, trying to see what had grabbed his attention in such a powerful way. But they were not able to see anything strange or out of the ordinary.

Before Peregrino's companions realized it, Peregrino's hypnotic state seized them, and they all stood in the middle of the road, unable to move as if turned to stone by Medusa, the Greek mythological monster. The two objects that had captured Peregrino's attention had entered the far right of his visual field furtively, like a pair of bashful ghosts. Those two ghosts were behind a young jacaranda tree stealthily calling for Peregrino's attention.

The bashful ghosts were the loose ends of a pair of red ribbons dancing and jumping up and down to the beat of the wind as if they were Chinese dancers.

Where have I seen that before?

Peregrino asked himself, but he was not able to remember. It did not matter how much he delved into his memory.

That bitter day on the battlefield, they scrambled his memories with an aluminum baseball bat to his head. And now, his memories were mixed up like the bagged pieces of a jigsaw puzzle.

Peregrino did not give up, and he dug frantically into his memory as if trying to unearth a bone he had buried there but could not remember where exactly.

Could it be one of those strange dreams that I often have but can never decipher? he asked himself. He continued digging into the part of his memory in charge of filing his dreams. Suddenly, hundreds of dreams passed before his mind's eye.

In one of those dreams, he saw a couple of ribbons dancing in the wind, which had colorful Japanese drawings that read, "January 17, 1995," and instantly and vividly, he saw the city of Kobe before, during, and after the big earthquake that had destroyed it, which he had dreamed a few days before it happened, but that was not what he was looking for.

Peregrino kept digging in his memory, and at the end of the list of dreams, he found something that seemed like half a dream and half a vision, where the sounds of the world became utterly silent. In that ambiguous dream, he saw himself inert on the ground, unable to hear the faintest sound; his eyelids were lead slowly veiling his eyes, and all he could feel was how life was dripping out of him.

Suddenly, Peregrino remembered where he had seen those red ribbons before. Those were the loose ends of the red ribbons he saw entwined in Julia's long braids that day when she and some of her friends wanted to take Bella's babies. And he saw those loose ends again when they were dancing in the wind while Julia was enjoying at a safe distance the massacre of dogs and street gang members, that day of the great battle. At that moment, it dawned on him that she was responsible for the deaths of his loved ones. Peregrino turned around to face his traveling companions and shouted, "For Pirate! For Ronaldinho! For Pure! For Dawn! For Niño! For Hayfield! For Eros!"

When Peregrino finished shouting, he looked at his companions with a vindictive expression and growling as loud as a Tasmanian devil, he turned around and ran toward the jacaranda tree behind which Julia was hiding.

Peregrino's companions bared their fangs and followed their leader, ready to attack anything or anyone, even though they didn't know where or who it was.

Lucky and Fortunato caught up with Peregrino and asked him where and who the enemy was. Peregrino explained briefly who Julia was and where she was hiding.

When Julia saw the pack of dogs coming directly at the tree behind which she was hiding, she knew they had discovered her hideout. Julia ran like a frightened fox to the nearest house and, screaming like a mad person, she banged desperately on the door, which was what she should have done the moment she recognized Lucky and Fortunato.

Fortunato said to Peregrino while running alongside him, "Please, Peregrino, I beg you, let that flesh be mine first." Peregrino nodded, and Fortunato turned into a fury of hair and teeth as he pounced on Julia.

Julia, remembering how those dogs had pierced her butt before, covered it with both her hands. Fortunato had no choice but to sink his teeth in the fat around her waist, which had taken the shape of the rear wheel of a Harley Davidson.

All the dogs pounced on Julia and were tearing her clothes and flesh to pieces. Suddenly, a burly albino man of slippery eyes, who's eyes move rapidly from left to right opened the door. When he saw the dogs taking advantage of the fact that Julia had enough flesh for everyone, he kicked Peregrino hard, so hard that he went flying to the ground on the naked avenue.

"No one does that to my brother and lives to tell the story," said Lucky. Before Lucky could finish the word story, the whole pack pounced on the albino man, who, paler than usual, was punching and kicking while backing into his house. Before he had the chance to close the door, Peregrino went flying over the heads of his mates and landed on the albino's chest, making him fall back on the floor.

The dogs made short work of the albino man, and when a woman came to his rescue with a broom, she was thrown to the floor by the dog's charge, where they took care of her. Even though they were street dogs, they were not killers; the pack only wanted to cause lots of pain, so they respected their faces and throat—even Julia's.

When the dogs finally calmed down, they headed for the exit, but Julia, being an ungrateful and mean woman, had closed the door and turned tail, leaving the people of the house at the mercy of the dogs.

The dogs looked for another way out but found none, so they went to lay down at the door. The albino man and his wife were so afraid that they stayed where the dogs left them on the floor, not wanting to move, not even a finger, not wanting to call the dogs' attention.

When the woman got tired of lying on the cold floor, she asked her husband to open the door for the dogs. "What!" exclaimed the man. "You want me to walk among all those teeth? Are you crazy, or do you have a screw loose?"

"Oh, you are so brave, so fearless, you are my hero," said the woman sarcastically. The man looked at his wife and nodded while smiling sardonically back at her.

"I guess you are thinking of adopting those dogs, right?" the woman said to her husband. When he smiled and nodded again, the woman knew she would have to go and open the door.

The woman got up slowly and painfully and approached the dogs while talking to them in a kind and sweet way. The dogs' ears pricked up and they took a good look at the woman. When they saw something that reminded them of María Margarita in her, they felt guilty for attacking the woman. They all approached her while wagging their tails, and immediately went to lick her injuries, which was their way of asking her forgiveness.

"You boys must be thirsty, and hungry," said the woman to the dogs, and she headed for the kitchen followed by her new friends. Once in the kitchen, she fed them all kinds of leftovers, and while the dogs ate avidly, the woman watched them with kind eyes.

When the dogs consumed the food and water, the woman said to them, "I guess it is time for you boys to go home, wherever that might be." Peregrino and company hugged and kissed the woman, thanking her for the food and water; the woman was moved by the dogs' show of affection and hugged and kissed them.

As the woman and her new friends came to the hallway leading to the exit door, she saw her husband holding the door wide open with his back to the wall. "Oh, my hero!" exclaimed the woman sarcastically. The man, with an ear-to-ear grin, nodded, and then he lifted his right foot so she could see the cowboy boots that had a sharp and shiny metal tip that he had put on while she was in the kitchen with the dogs.

"No, please! I beg you, don't hurt them," the woman cried out.

"Okay, I won't, I promise," said the man. As the dogs went out one by one, the man said to the dogs, "Thank you for visiting us." When Ares, who was the last one to get out of the house, was halfway out the door, the man kicked him with all his might, sinking the metal tip up Ares' behind. "Visiting time is over, stinking mutt," said the man as he slammed the door.

Poor Ares went out flying like a football. The pain in his rear end was so terrible that it seemed to him that the gears that produced all the sounds of the world had suddenly come to a stop. Ares flew to the naked avenue in complete silence, unable to utter even a muffled screech.

When Ares landed on the naked avenue, he lifted his tail and rubbed his rear end in the warm, soft sand as if he were trying to put out a fire that was coming out of his butt. The terrible pain he was feeling gave him the certainty that his bones were on fire and that at any moment, his eyes would explode out of his skull.

All of Ares' friends, seeing him cry in pain, quickly went to help him in the only way they knew, licking. And lick they did. While Ares lay on his back, his friends licked his ears, face, rear end, and genitals.

All that licking replaced Ares' pain for sensual pleasure. An overwhelming tickling coursed through his body back and forth. Not knowing how to handle that feeling, Ares got up and then squatted down to pee like a female dog, which gave him tremendous satisfaction.

Evening was falling. The sun god's dying light rays had set the mountains on the horizon on fire. The naked avenue with its melange of the beautiful colors of the bougainvillea and the light blue of the jacaranda trees was trying to match the splendor of the setting sun. The dogs had regained their cheerful pace and were enjoying their freedom.

The exotic smells coming out of the kitchens of the endless row of houses were enticing the dogs' sense of smell, but the dogs were resisting the temptation to go and beg for scraps. After all, they knew that their freedom entailed that sometimes they must go hungry.

Peregrino was leading the pack. He was walking a few steps ahead of his traveling companions and was trying to understand the overwhelming feelings that were robbing him of the happiness of that moment. Somehow, those feelings were making him feel responsible for the lives of those following his steps.

Just before the last crepuscular rays disappeared completely, Peregrino stopped walking and turned around to look at his adventure mates before darkness enveloped them in its arms.

The sunset's last diffused light rays made Peregrino see an iridescent aura around each of his companions. In a fraction of a second, he saw them without their doggy outfits, without their terrestrial suits. That gave him a fleeting glimpse of the beauty that hides within all living beings.

Peregrino's traveling mates stopped their cheerful pace and looked at him, and then they looked at the road and the trees behind him, half expecting to see an enemy of those that only he could discover.

Peregrino's heart, overflowing with happiness thanks to the fleeting glimpse he had, stared in amazement at his companions. And without realizing it, his feelings came out loud through his mouth. "Bella the beautiful! Lucky, my beloved brother! Fortunato the daring! Ares and Nikus, the dauntless! I love you all."

No sooner had Peregrino finished saying how much he loved his companions, when out of nowhere appeared Guapo right next to him and said, "This is as far as you go. You are coming with me." All the dogs pounced on Guapo simultaneously. Guapo sneered at them inwardly and made them move in slow motion so he would have plenty of time to vanish.

When Guapo was about to escape, the red glow in Lucky's eyes caught his attention, and at the same time, he heard the saying, "Memento Mori!" come out of Lucky's mouth like a distant echo. And that made Guapo remember the day Death turned him into a herald. Death warned him to beware of a dog with a red glow in its eyes that would be saying, "Memento Mori," because that would be the only dog that can send you to Hell.

When Guapo realized that Lucky was the dog he was supposed to be wary of, he became utterly distracted and forgot to keep the slow-motion effect going. Lucky took advantage of Guapo's momentary distraction, caught him by the neck, and shook him violently. Guapo's head rolled to the ground where it turned to dust, and so did the rest of his body, and that was the end of Guapo.

Lucky's companions looked at him in awe and could not believe what he had just done. "You just killed Guapo!" Nikus exclaimed.

"No," said Peregrino. "He was already dead. Lucky just got rid of a wicked spirit."

"What power do you have to be able to do that?" Nikus asked Lucky.

Before Lucky had a chance to answer Nikus' question, Bella said, "The power of love and goodness. Lucky is capable of so much love and so much good. Only love can defeat hate. Only good can defeat evil."

"Hats off to you, my lady," said Nikus. "Those are indeed beautiful words of wisdom."

"Thank you," said Bella, bowing graciously.

Nikus and Bella joined the others who had Lucky on the ground and were biting him playfully to show him how much they loved and admired him. The astonishment and excitement for Lucky's incredible feat gradually diminished. The friends sat on the ground thinking about the day's experiences and fell silent. Following a short silence, Peregrino got up from the ground and, facing Ares and Nikus, said to them, "You are no longer our friends."

"What?" exclaimed Nikus.

"From now on, you are family, and as members of this family, you deserve to know what happened to the rest of our family, and you must hear their story."

Peregrino told them about Niño and Mona.

Then he shared Ronaldinho and Cinderella's story. As well as Pepita's, Mariano's, Pirate's, Pure's, Dawn's, Hayfield's, the new Niño's, Eros', Alexander's, Cindy's, Anaximenes', and Anaximander's stories.

When Peregrino finished telling their stories, he said solemnly, "We shall never forget our dead ones, and we shall never forget those that went with Mariano.

Let us hope our paths cross soon." Everyone nodded in agreement. When Ares and Nikus were welcome as family members with hugs and kisses, everyone was as happy as can be. Peregrino, looking at Fortunato, asked him, "Are you ready to be the pack's leader?" "I sure am," he said proudly.

"Okay then, you are now the pack's leader for the rest of the night. From this moment on, your wish is our command. What do you wish us to do?"

"I think we had enough excitement for a day. I say we all huddle and go to sleep."

They huddled by the side of the road under the starry sky and slept and dreamed the dreams dogs usually have.

THE NEW LITTER

The sun god rose rosy-cheeked behind the mountains on the horizon, turning to gold everything it touched. Pepita knew it would be a sunny and warm morning, perfect for a trek down the garbage dump and a long walk in the jungle.

"Okay, boys and girls," Pepita said to her new litter of puppies. "Today is the day you have been waiting for; I am taking you to Peregrino's two worlds." The young pups screamed with joy and wagged their tails excitedly, as they followed Pepita to the garbage dump.

If there is a heaven at the end of the road, it belongs to the people who truly love dogs.

9 798880 396580